A **Shot** in the **Bark**

A Dog Park Mystery

by

C. A. Newsome

This is a work of fiction. All of the characters, places and events portrayed in this book are either products of the author's imagination or are used fictitiously.

A Shot in the Bark

Cover art by Carol Ann Newsome

Published by
CreateSpace Independent Publishing Platform

ISBN-13: 978-1481026703
ISBN-10: 1481026704

To the two and four-footed friends who share my mornings.

Acknowledgments

Many, many thanks to Lou Marti for being my main sounding board and critic while I was writing this book, and to Angie Hall for her colorful feedback on the MS. Thank you Mom for editing and for always believing in me. Special thanks to Tom Sansalone, John Cunningham, Anna Woo, Nick "Jose" Misch and Lou Marti for allowing me to base characters on them. Thanks to Anna Woo and Pat North for their eternal, unwavering support.

Prologue

Fifteen years ago

He had to go. Could she do it? Years with this man were endurable while he was pursuing his ambitions, working long hours and out of town for days at a time. Then retirement brought his domineering ways home and the man who was a big fish in a very big pond now thrashed around in her little puddle, making life miserable with his endless demands.

Potassium Chloride was virtually undetectable. It mimicked heart attacks, and he'd already had two. No one would notice the injection site because he took daily insulin shots. Could she sneak it into his syringe? Could she set it up so he would give it to himself while she was away? But the syringe would have a chemical residue. And if potassium changed the color of insulin, he'd notice.

What would deflect suspicion? If she were gone when it happened, she could arrange an alibi. That would mean an unattended death and maybe an autopsy. If she were present and had to face EMTs, could she pull off acting dazed and grieving? Could she time it right, the call to 911?

She recalled the Harris case, which blew up because he delayed the 911 call too long. His wife's skin was dry when the EMTs arrived and he had cleaned up the bathroom. Too clean. She was sure he had to clean it up because his wife thrashed around in the bath while he was holding her under. The floor was bone dry. No puddles from a distraught husband dragging her out of the tub. And he drained the tub. Was there something in the water to make her sleepy? Only her hair had been wet when the EMTs arrived, a fact that led to months of controversy in the press and in the courts, racking up thousands of dollars in expert witness testimony. Such a small thing and it led to disaster. Could anyone remember everything to do at a time like that?

Her thoughts returned to the man she'd lived with for so long. Her love was reduced to grinding resentment. He was a miserable man in a life where he no longer had a purpose, where his sphere of influence was reduced from affecting thousands over the years to this kingdom with only one citizen to rule.

His only joy was making her even more miserable than he was. He would be better dead. Careful planning was required. Could she pull it off? Could she do it?

Chapter 1

Saturday, May 7

"How did I get mixed up with such a loser, Anna?" Lia's question somehow managed to be simultaneously earnest and rhetorical. The lithe, thirty-ish artist posed this question as she and her friend perched on top of a picnic table at the Mount Airy Dog Park, watching their furry children at play.

Anna, wise in the ways of the heart, kept silent. Like all good cops and therapists, she knew a void invited unburdening. She was a sturdy, middle-aged woman of medium height, with a square face and thin lips. Dark brows hovered over intense eyes of an indeterminate color. Nature had gifted her with hair that went pale gold instead of grey, and it waved softly just above her shoulders. It was her one beauty. Like everything in her life, its display was understated.

Lia sighed and ruffled the ears of Chewy, her silver Miniature Schnauzer. Satisfied, Chewy took off for another tour of the park perimeter. Lia tracked his jaunty trot with fretful green eyes while she gathered her thoughts. "I know better. Mom went through the same damn thing with her second husband. Handsome, talented, and just needed a little help to manifest his brilliant potential. Ha!" She bent her head forward while she gave a pat to a passing lab. Summer-streaked chestnut hair poured over her shoulders, curtaining her expressive eyes. She chewed on her bottom lip and picked at the fringe on her paint-splattered cut-offs.

Anna gently posed her question. "You've been seeing him for, what, almost a year now? What's upsetting you today?"

"Nothing's upsetting me. That is, nothing's changed. Nothing's improved, nothing's different. He always acts like I'm this big muse, and he says he's writing like crazy but he's just rearranging deck chairs on the Titanic." She gusted a sigh while rolling her eyes. "I take that back. He's not rearranging them, he's tossing them into a big pile and pouring gasoline on them. It's a funeral pyre on a sinking ship."

"So what brought this on today?" Anna asked.

"I read his latest revisions yesterday. Thinking about it kept me up most of the night. The manuscript was nearly finished when I met him a year ago. It's no closer to being finished now than it was then." Lia paused. "Really, it's further away. His revisions are chopping it up so it's disjointed and unpublishable. He says he needs to cut pages, but he'll need to add another 50 pages to pull together all the new material he's added. He's killed the pace and it's lost its freshness. He's overworked the good parts until they just lay there, dead and stinking to high heaven." Lia ended her rant and sat back, arms folded.

"That's quite an image."

"Anna, it's pure road kill. I told him, 'You can't sell something if you never finish it. You can't finish it if you keep adding new elements that mean you have to rewrite the whole damn thing. You're not curing cancer here, you're just trying to entertain people.'"

"Good thing he's a writer, not a painter. He can go back to an earlier version of the manuscript when he comes to his senses."

4

"That's just it," Lia's voice took on a disgusted edge. "He's been overwriting the file all along. I set up his computer and showed him how to save different versions of the book as he made changes, and he blew it off. He said it was too much trouble."

Anna considered this. "There's software that can retrieve it, isn't there?"

"There isn't if Paul offers to defrag your computer while you're having beers. It's gone. For good. Honey! Stop digging! Right! Now!" Lia's anger made this reprimand sharper than it should have been.

Honey usually deserved her name. Today she was busily enlarging a hole created by an earlier dog park visitor and quickly losing her sweetheart status. Chewy found this very amusing and sniffed the dirt pile, emerging with dirty paws and a clump of sod on his pert nose.

"Honey! I said STOP!" This time the handsome Golden Retriever looked up, her expression sheepish. She returned to Lia in a penitent slouch and placed one dirt caked paw in Lia's lap in a plea for forgiveness. Lia looked down at the dark smudges on her shorts. "And I thought Goldens were the perfect breed." She scratched behind Honey's ears and gave her a kiss on the top of her head.

Anna laughed, a merry tinkling full of good humor and empathy. "At least you have the sense to dress for the park. Not like some I might name."

Lia noticed the older woman's eyes flick over to the pair sitting at a picnic table several yards away. Lia knew she wasn't talking about Jim. Jim's couture was comfortable, well-used and rumpled, like his face and personality. It was the coifed grand-dame deftly touching his arm that drew this bit of spite from Anna.

5

"I miss Jim, too. I'm sorry I ever introduced them. Catherine's had her claws out for him ever since. And she never would have looked at him twice if I hadn't raved about what a great friend he was. Now every time I'm around him, she does everything she can to distract him from me."

Catherine Laroux and her twin Pomeranians had appeared three months earlier. Caesar and Cleo (Anna, Bailey and Lia privately called them "Prissy" and "Poopsy") didn't need much exercise. Catherine needed escape from her husband, and attention. Lots of attention. Any attention would do, and she got it with flattering focus and playing the damsel in distress. Whether it was people who slighted her, symptoms she couldn't decipher, or appliances she didn't understand, Catherine always found a reason to seek help and advice. She had a consummate talent for making her needs more important than anything else that might be happening. The women caught on quickly. The men, typically, when faced with the full brunt of femininity, were clueless.

"It's amazing, isn't it?" Lia continued. "How many problems can one person have at 8:00 a.m. in the dog park?"

This time Anna responded with a ladylike snort. "Now, now. Let's collect our furry children and see if they might like to chase some balls."

Anna's handsome and mannerly Tibetan Mastiff, CarGo (as in "Car! Go!"), was stately and full of humor. He was black and tan and always well-groomed. Like his mistress, he deplored fussiness and remained aloof from drama. He galloped up - gallop is the only word that would work. At 125 pounds, CarGo could be mistaken for a small horse. His one bad habit was jumping up, and with paws on shoulders, looking humans in the eyes. In moments of whimsey, Anna considered teaching him ballroom dancing.

His canine radar infallible, CarGo was ready as soon as Anna pulled her "flinger" from her bag. Anna expertly launched two balls in the air. CarGo beelined after a line-drive, Chewy yapping at his heels while Honey considered a high lob, bolting when its trajectory became apparent. She leapt up to snag it out of the air before CarGo pounced on his own grounder.

Anna turned to look at Lia. "I love watching them play. I don't even mind the slobber. So what will you do about him?"

"Luthor?" responded Lia, not thrown by the non-sequitur. "What I always do, I suppose. Withdraw.

"People who accomplish anything are finishers. They don't whine or make excuses. They might adjust their course a bit, but they don't suddenly decide to switch destinations. All of a sudden, Luthor doesn't know what kind of book he's writing. This is 18 months into the thing, and he hasn't decided who the killer is, or if he ought to be writing a police procedural instead of a psychological thriller. Drives me crazy. Once I figured he was never going to finish the book, I lost all feeling for him."

"Over a book?"

"Over his lack of direction and his pretense that he's actually doing something. I can't be with someone who hasn't entered the real world. Sooner or later, they wind up turning on me like it's my fault they haven't accomplished anything."

"Poor girl. I'm so glad he never moved in"

"That would have been a mistake. I'm dreading this as it is. Oh, Gawd. Here he comes."

It was the sound of a perforated muffler that drew Lia's attention to the parking lot. Luthor had named the rattle-trap Corolla "William" because it had "suffered the slings and arrows of outrageous fortune." Lia thought "Shakes-Gear" was more to the point.

Luthor Morrisey was a handsome man, blond and tall. His hair was deliberately unkempt, and his clothes, while expensive, were unpressed and tossed on. 19th Century Romanticism overlaid with a patina of 21st Century Artist Grunge. Lia reckoned he'd coasted on his looks and self-serving artistic sensitivity for too long, that and his advance guard, Viola, a lovable but occasionally schitzy Border Collie mix whose silky fur drew admirers. In an act of compassion that Lia suspected slayed the hearts of many women before her, Luthor had spotted the traumatized puppy in a February ice storm and spent over an hour coaxing it to warmth and safety. But animal rescue only gets you so far. She mused, "I'll miss the dog."

"Lia!" Luthor yelled, waving a long arm over head.

"As if I didn't figure out he was here when the car was a mile away," she muttered.

"Now, Lia, have pity. He doesn't know what's coming."

"No, he doesn't have a clue. That's the problem." Lia mustered a limp half-smile (or was it a grimace?) and went to meet him with dread in her heart.

Anna watched as Lia ignored Luthor's outstretched arms and perched on a table. Her crossed arms confused Viola, who expected hugs. Lia's defensive posture must have sunk in, Anna noted, as Luthor's stance suddenly became aggressive. Anna continued to watch the performance as Luthor's voice became audible over the distance and elevated in pitch. She could almost, but not quite, understand what he was saying.

"Third time a charm?" a familiar voice asked.

Anna turned to look at Jim. The retired engineer was a short man with kind eyes and a shaggy beard. Anna thought, not for the first time, how much he resembled Treebeard, the ancient ent in *Lord of the Rings*. "I hope so, the other breakups didn't stick. I hope this one does. This is wearing her down."

"Is she going to be okay?"

"Sooner or later. Lia's resilient. But I'd so hoped he would make her happy." Anna craned her neck further. "What happened to your girlfriend?"

"Girlfriend? Catherine? She just needed some advice. She's not my girlfriend. Fleece is the only woman in my life." Jim referred to his beloved Border Collie, who was currently attempting to herd a pair of Lab pups.

"You're too kind, Jim." Or too blind, she privately thought.

A tall redhead with chin-length hair joined them. Bailey had the kind of figure that photographed well because she was always fifteen pounds underweight. In real life, she came off as gawky. She had an open face with mildly popped eyes, and a nose that an unkind person might call 'beaky.' She had a hesitant smile, with the left side quirking up while the right remained undecided. "So do you think this will be the end?" Bailey gestured to the discordant pair with a long, graceful hand that should have been pouring tea or playing piano. Ironically, her fingers were always callused and nicked from her job as a self-employed gardener.

"I hope so," Anna responded, "but I don't think he'll let her go easily and she's already stressing over that garden you two are building for Catherine. I'm so angry at Luthor, he should be supporting her so she can do her work, not expecting her to nursemaid him while he pretends to be a writer."

"Support her?" Bailey looked amused. "He can't even put gas in his car."

"Not that. She does okay by herself. I meant cook her dinner, rub her feet instead of expecting her to rub his all the time. He's not the one standing on a concrete floor all day painting. Why is it men always think their needs are more important, Jim?"

9

"Anna, you know I'm not going to touch that." Jim looked at her sideways and put up both palms in a universal request for peace.

The sound of a car door slamming brought them back to the drama at hand. Squealing tires announced Luthor's departure.

"I don't think he can afford to lose any rubber," Jim said dryly. "He could blow out a tire going down Montana Avenue."

"Don't say that!" Bailey interjected. "If he dies on that hill, she'll feel guilty and paint his picture forever. If he lives, she'll still feel guilty, she'll be rubbing his feet in the hospital, and she'll still paint his picture forever. Either way, it'll destroy her career because who wants to buy a hundred paintings of Luthor? We'll never finish Catherine's garden. I won't get paid and I'll wind up starving."

~ ~ ~

Sunday, May 8, 4:00 a.m.

Lia couldn't say she was up early because she'd never been to bed. Luthor's recriminations and endless phone calls echoed in her head all night. Weary, she'd unplugged the phone at 1:00 a.m. At 1:30 she'd taken a long, hot soak in Epsom Salts, her favored cure for insomnia. It hadn't worked.

Luthor probably started leaving nasty messages on her cell phone at exactly 1:05 a.m., but as usual she didn't know where her cell was. She hated the damn thing and only kept it because there was no phone at the studio. That's where it probably was.

She hoped her phone wasn't over by the south wall. She thought of Jason, an illegal loft-liver on the other side of that wall. Better buy him a twelve-pack. Make it imported. I bet the

10

ringing has been driving him crazy. If I'm lucky, the battery's dead. She pictured Jason, enraged by the noise, punching a hole in the dry wall to retrieve her phone and fling it out a window. She winced. At least then I wouldn't have to listen to the messages. How many were there? One three hour rant? A hundred one-word nuisance calls? How quickly can you call and leave a message? Two minutes? At two minutes a message and three hours, ninety messages? What are the limits on the in-box? She hoped for Jason's sake it was one very long message, or that the battery was dead. How long would it take to delete ninety messages?

Tired of her head spinning, Lia pulled on sweats and grabbed her keys. The soft jingle had Chewy and Honey beating her to the door. "You guys don't miss a trick, do you? Up for some pre-dawn prowling?" She snapped leashes to their collars. "Shall we walk this time? It's only a mile-and-a-half, what do you think?"

Lia learned to appreciate baker's hours years ago when an outdoor mural had her working in the pre-dawn dark so she could project her design on the wall. Her friends were horrified, convinced her body would turn up months later in Mill Creek. But Lia loved how quiet the world was at 4:00 a.m. Inside at 4:00 a.m., your brain would be in over-drive. The world outside was silent at 4:00 a.m. You never realized how noisy houses were until you went outside in the dead of night. The quiet calmed her mind. Outside was peace. No pain, no drama, and she could let everything go.

Lia hit her stride. Not a power walk, but quick and steady through the darkness. She watched her shadow change direction and shape as she passed under street lights. The rhythmic motion eased her. Honey and Chewy trotted obediently beside her. Her head started to clear and she began to relax. This is the ticket. One and a half miles to the park, let the dogs run around a bit, back home, fry up some potatoes and eggs. It's Sunday, no need to plug the phone in. Play some Mozart. Do the crossword. Don't think. Go back to bed. Yes.

She turned down Westwood Northern Boulevard, jogging down the hill for the last half-mile. Honey and Chewy barked happily. "Shush!" she admonished, laughing as the last of the tension poured out.

She slowed to a walk as she turned into the parking lot. She was looking forward to sitting on a table, looking up at the sky and watching the stars until the rising sun blinked them out. Then she saw the dark hulk at the far end. The familiar silhouette had her grinding her teeth. What was Luthor doing here? He couldn't have known she was coming this early, could he? Or had he been parked outside her apartment and seen her leave? Was he stalking her? But surely she would have heard him. She would have heard his muffler, anyway.

Shit. Shit. Shit. Damn. Her mental cussing became a litany as she angrily strode towards the car. Then she thought better and turned towards the utility road leading up to the entrance corral. For whatever reason, Luthor had not gotten out of his car. She didn't want to be freaking out in the parking lot, upsetting the dogs so close to the street.

So she climbed the hill, passed through the fenced corral, and released Honey and Chewy. She pulled a rag out of her pocket and wiped the dew from a spot on her favorite table top and clambered up. She sat facing the parking lot, no longer thinking about stars or sunrise. The car was still. Surely he'd heard the dogs barking? Maybe he'd passed out drunk. Maybe he just came so he could sit there and snub her. Like how would she ever know she was being snubbed if she couldn't see him doing it.

The minutes passed. Honey and Chewy whuffed softly as they made their nocturnal investigations. False dawn appeared over the ridge. Shit. The litany began again, tired now. Shit. Shit. Shit. Damn. She couldn't put it off any longer. Her brief spell of serenity was broken and beyond repair. Trudging back down the hill, she wondered what she could possibly say to Luthor that she hadn't already said.

By the time she hit the parking lot, she was pissed. Was he going to spoil her favorite place for her now? Were they going to have to divvy it up, take different shifts, different quadrants, different friends? If they did that would he respect it and leave her be? Somehow she doubted it.

"Luthor!" His name was a sharp retort in the darkness, like a pistol shot. "What the hell are you doing? Why can't you just give me some space?"

The Corolla remained silent. Was he in the car at all? Had she been fuming for nothing? Maybe he drove it here last night and it broke down. Or was he passed out? He didn't normally drink alone, but he might have made an exception.

She neared the passenger side and spied a dark form leaning back in the driver's seat. Damn. Looks like Door Number Two. She wrenched the door open and the absence of alcohol fumes hit her the same time the overhead light did.

~ ~ ~

Lia huddled on the picnic table. In the telepathic way of all dogs, Honey and Chewy sensed her distress and had her sandwiched between them. Radios crackled in the distance. Yellow tape fluttered as police set up a perimeter.

Jim handed her a cup of coffee and she cradled it between her palms, leached warmth into skin chilled by horror. It was Jim who found her at daybreak, hugging the dogs, rocking in shock, Jim who called District Five, and Jim who sent Anna for coffee at the closest UDF.

She looked at him, pleading. She had a stray thought, that his compassionate face belonged on a religious icon. Something Italian, from one of the Catholic sects that embraced poverty. He could have been a Franciscan monk. Maybe Saint Francis himself.

"Lia, you're not responsible. It was his choice. And it was his choice to do it where you might find him. He knew you're often first up here in the morning. I'm sorry it happened, but that was wrong of him. It was hateful to put you through this."

Tears started to seep out of Lia's eyes. Anna leaned over and wrapped an arm around her. "I'm so sorry, Sweetie, it shouldn't have happened. Not like this."

Lia took a sip of coffee. "Hazelnut. You knew to get hazelnut creamer for me." Her mouth quirked sadly.

"Of course," Anna responded kindly.

"What do you mean I can't come in?" The strident voice drifted up from the parking lot. "I have to come in. Those are my friends!"

Lia looked towards the police barrier and groaned.

"I'm sure Catherine is worried about you," Jim said.

"Hush," Anna snapped. "Maybe somewhere in her tiny little heart she's thinking about Lia, but that won't stop her from making this all about her. She's already well on her way."

"Now, Anna, that's uncalled for," Jim responded.

"Stop it!"

The guilty pair looked at Lia, taken aback by her outburst.

"I can't take the bickering," she pleaded.

"We're sorry, Lia," Anna responded. "We won't do it anymore. Looks like the police are taking care of Catherine for you." They watched as Catherine's Lexus turned around and pulled out. A lone figure worked its way up the access road and through the corral, approaching their table.

"No uniform," Jim observed. "Must be a detective."

He was tall, maybe two inches over six feet. Lean, with an easy stride. Longish, dark hair. A pleasant face with slightly droopy eyes. Like Paul McCartney. Puppy dog eyes that might turn into Basset Hound eyes in old age, though Sir Paul wasn't looking too shabby these days. His golf shirt and khaki slacks reminded Lia she was still in her sweats. And very shortly, the heat was going to turn on like flipping a switch.

"Hi. You found the body?" The inquiry was soft, as if he was afraid of startling her.

Lia nodded dumbly as she stared at the ground, having a sudden flash of Michael Douglas gently coaxing Kathleen Turner out from under a bus in a Central American jungle. What was that film? Something about a stone?

"Lia Anderson, is it?"

Another mute nod.

"We had to send your friend away. I hope that doesn't upset you."

Lia's mouth quirked, a sign of life. His calm tone steadied her. She took a deep breath and shook her head, still looking down. "It's alright. Are you a detective? Jim said you must be a detective."

"Yes, Detective Dourson. Peter Dourson."

"Detective, can I ask you a question?"

"Sure, go ahead."

"How long will I be stuck here?"

"We're not sure at this point. Is there somewhere you have to be?"

"No, but this is strange, you know?"

"I know. We need to ask you some questions. We've been waiting for the Victim Advocate to show up."

"It's okay, we don't need to wait. I've got Jim and Anna."

15

"Are you sure? Do you have someone to be with you when you leave here?"

"I can take her home, Detective. I'll look after her." Anna brushed a strand of hair out of Lia's face. "She won't be alone."

"All right then. Jim and Anna. You would be Jim McDonald? You called this in?"

"Yep. This is Anna Lawrence. She got here right after I did."

"And what time was that?"

"Around six."

Dourson raised his eyebrows.

"All the dogs know is that it's daylight. They could care less about what time it is."

Dourson smiled at that. "Is that everyday?"

"Pretty much."

Dourson turned to Lia, "You were here before that. When did you get here?"

"O-dark-thirty? I don't know. I left the house a little after four and we walked up here."

"Who was with you?"

"Just the dogs, Honey and Chewy."

"That's pretty early."

"I couldn't sleep."

"How long does it take you to walk up here?"

"Twenty, twenty-five minutes."

"So does four-thirty sound about right?"

"I guess, I don't know. I misplaced my cell. I don't wear a watch."

"So what happened when you got here?"

"I saw the car and I was pissed."

"Pissed? How come?"

"Didn't they tell you?"

"Tell me what? What am I missing?"

"Officer," Anna interjected. "Detective, he was her boyfriend. She broke up with him yesterday."

"I'm sorry."

Lia's tears started again. "I'm sorry, too. So sorry."

Dourson was gentle. "Lia, are you okay to do this?"

"I don't want to wait."

"Okay, tell me what happened after you got here. Take your time."

"I was pissed." Lia restarted her story and haltingly recounted events up to the time she threw open the car door.

"What did you see?"

"Blood, all over. The back window, the seat. He was just lying there in it with his mouth open."

"This is really important. Did you touch anything?"

"No, no. The passenger side door handle, that's it."

"Why the passenger side door?"

"It was closest."

"Detective Dourson surveyed the trio. "Did anyone else touch anything?"

"I looked in because she was just staring and wouldn't say anything," Jim volunteered, "I didn't touch the car."

"How about you, Anna?"

"I didn't go near the car."

Dourson turned back to Lia. "Tell me about the breakup. Was this your idea?"

Lia dully cited the hours of phone calls and recriminations laced with wheedling, begging and vicious profanity. No, she couldn't remember exactly what he said. The verbal barrage flooded her, leaving behind a vile tone, but no quotes. She did recall he'd called her "Angel" in one sentence, and used the "C" word in the next.

"That's why I couldn't sleep, it was so nasty. I couldn't get it out of my head." She looked up at him then, finally, her jade eyes glistening and her lashes damp. "Was it suicide, Detective?"

Dourson paused for a moment, struck by mossy eyes that reminded him of cool green walks in Kentucky hollows. They were complimented by a soft, vulnerable mouth and those slightly aloof cheekbones. He noticed a slight dent in her chin, as if someone had pressed a thumb in it and left an imprint. Her hair was bound up in a clip. Spiraling tendrils escaped, emphasizing her long neck and reinforcing her fragility. He mentally shook his head and focussed on her question. "It's early to say."

"I'm sure you're not allowed to say, anyway."

"That, too, but really, it's too early to know for sure."

"I was so angry. I wanted him gone, but I didn't want that."

"I know."

"Do you?" she pleaded.

"Yeah, I think so," he said, as his heart broke for her.

Dourson collected contact information for Lia, Jim and Anna, and for Luthor's parents. Anna led Lia out to her SUV while Jim followed along with the dogs. Dourson picked up Lia's abandoned coffee. It was still almost full. He smelled hazelnut. He dumped it in the trash.

~ ~ ~

She remembered most the explosion of blood, the mess, and the blow-back speckling her clothes and skin. There would be plenty of time to burn her clothes, and the neighbors would just assume she was grilling out. She'd encourage that impression by dumping on

Liquid Smoke. The police might never ask questions, not if they bought the suicide scenario she created.

She'd disliked doing it this way. Luthor had no convenient health issues to exploit, nor did he care for outdoor activities that could be manipulated into accidents. He had only one obvious weakness, and that was his dependence on Lia.

She pondered the cell phone in her hand. It had been so easy to lift from Lia's tote. Easier still to lure Luthor with a text message. But what to do with it? Return it to Lia? Destroy it? It would be easiest to destroy it and Lia would probably figure she'd lost it. It wouldn't be too difficult to return, just drop it behind the driver's seat of her Volvo. The windows were always open for the dogs. But she'd have to remove those final text messages, and if the police came asking questions, possession of the phone would cause Lia problems.

If she got the phone back, Lia would feel compelled to access all of Luthor's messages from last night. She could still do it without the phone, but would she bother? Too bad there was no way for her to find out what was on voicemail without it being flagged that it had been accessed. Luthor's messages shouldn't be incriminating. How could they be? Checking messages would tip Lia off that someone else had her phone, and that wouldn't be good at all.

It had taken more time to dig Luthor's phone out of his jacket and pull off those last texts than it had to kill him. It had been delicate going, putting it back. She'd felt horribly exposed even though trees blocked the view of the parking lot from the street. But she couldn't have Luthor's phone missing. That would be a tip-off. And if police ruled it suicide, they wouldn't bother to pull the phone records, would they?

Such a nasty job, all the way around. She disliked guns, disliked blood, and disliked loose ends. She looked at the loose end in her palm and smiled with sudden inspiration. Insurance. She'd leave the messages and hang onto it for now. Just in case.

Chapter 2

Monday, May 9

Lia woke up late the next day. Or rather, Chewy and Honey woke her up, tag teaming her with kisses and bright yips, as if being happy could get her out of bed. Two nights of no sleep, then she spent yesterday either comatose or crying. Anna had hung out in the next room, checking in occasionally to bring her some tea or food. She remembered a grilled cheese sandwich she couldn't eat. She remembered a confused Chewy snuffling her tears as if to figure out what they were.

It was 8:00. The morning shift at the dog park would be in full swing. No matter how she was feeling, Honey and Chewy still needed to go run.

The Mount Airy Dog Park had two fenced areas, the smaller designated for small dogs. Few people used it because it had little shade and most of the small dogs liked chasing the big dogs on the other side. But it was a good place to go if you wanted to be alone.

Lia perched on the table nearest the fence, the only one with shade. She considered the group next door. Since the park had been closed yesterday morning, she figured everyone was peppering Anna and Jim with questions about the shooting. Terry Dunn, a robust reincarnation of Teddy Roosevelt, drew a line in the air with his finger. He appeared to be calculating the trajectory of the bullet while Marie Woo and Nadine Moyers watched.

Marie was a petite, feisty, first-generation Asian-American whose feathery, jet-black hair was accented with an eye-popping forelock in ever-changing hues. She had her head canted so that this month's magenta bangs flopped, the way they always did when she was getting ready to challenge Terry. Her unmarked skin had an ageless look; Marie refused to enlighten anyone on that point. In contrast to her firecracker personality, Marie's face was inscrutable. The only indication of her feelings was the degree of tilt to her head. Right now, the tilt was slight and her chin was down. Her interest was academic, not personal.

Nadine was a sporty grandmother with sprightly blue eyes and snowy, boy-cut hair. Nadine could often be spotted power-walking back and forth across the park with her arms pumping determinedly and Rufus trotting dutifully behind. She had paused in this morning's trek to nowhere to catch the gossip. She touched Jim's arm with one hand, the other going to her mouth in a gesture of horror.

Catherine, wearing a fuchsia faux-silk jogging outfit, fussed with her Pomeranians. She looked up, glaring daggers at Nadine.

Funny, Lia thought, I can't hear a word they're saying and I still know exactly what's going on.

Anna and CarGo detached from the group, followed by a tall man Lia didn't know. As she approached, Anna waved, "Lia! Look who showed up! It's Detective Peter! Look who he brought with him!"

Lia squinted and sure enough, she recognized the rangy figure. She looked lower and spotted Viola dancing around CarGo in a vain attempt to get the mastiff to play.

"Detective Peter, is it?"

"Lia, you know we can't be formal here, and he's off duty now. I'm so glad you're up. I was going to check in on you when we were done here."

"So, Detective Peter, what brings you out here?" Lia asked

"Viola's staying with me for now. I thought she would like to play with her friends. She's been a bit anxious."

"How did you wind up with her?"

"Luthor's parents were less than enthusiastic about stepping up for her. I figured I could look after her until we found someone to take her."

"Yeah, the old man's allergic. So he says."

"I thought there might be a friend somewhere who would want her if I hung onto her for a few days. Otherwise, it was the shelter. So I'm letting folks know she needs a home."

"Thank you for taking her in. I don't know if I'm up to taking on another dog. I'll have to think about it."

"Sure, just let me know. By the way, we may have some questions for you, just some loose ends to tie up. Can you stop in at District Five tomorrow? Or I can come to you if you prefer."

"That would be nice. You can never park at District Five."

"It's a pain, I know. Any time in particular?"

Arrangements made, Anna and Lia watched the detective head for the parking lot with his capering dark shadow.

"That's a nice young man," Anna observed.

"Are we talking a little cougar action here?"

"Not a bad idea, but I suspect he might have a different agenda."

"Oh, really?"

~ ~ ~

There are rules to getting away with murder.

Rule Number One: You can't confide in anyone. Nobody. Not ever. Secrets are ticking time bombs. It's hard to keep a secret, but when it's your secret, you have every reason to keep it. Even with his mistakes, Harris should have gotten away with murder after two mistrials. Then a witness came forward. She claimed Harris bragged about killing his wife. A not-very-credible witness, as it turned out, but it gave the prosecution the chance to correct the mistakes they made in the first two trials. Then they nailed him the third time around.

Talking is tempting fate. That's my mantra. I don't like keeping secrets, and sometimes the pressure builds and I sit quietly and meditate. I repeat 100, 1,000 times, "Talking is tempting fate," while I close my eyes and imagine the color orange to remind myself how ghastly it looks on me.

Rule Number Two: Never kill when you are angry. You make mistakes when you're angry, the biggest mistake being the desire for violence. Violence leaves behind evidence of violence, the biggest piece of evidence being that the death was, in fact, murder and not an accident or natural causes.

Rule Number Three: Make it look like something else. An accident, suicide, a health condition, anything but murder. You can't be convicted for a crime if no one knows one occurred.

Rule Number Four: Plan, plan, plan. Rehearse, rehearse, rehearse. You have to review and practice your plan enough to find all the holes, and there are always holes. It has to be second nature because the mind often blanks when stressed. You've got to be programmed in case fear strikes. When your mind blanks, you've got to go on auto-pilot.

Rule Number Five: Never repeat yourself. Don't kill two husbands, two bosses, or two landlords. Never kill two people the same way. Repeating creates patterns and patterns create suspicion.

Avoid connections between victims because connections will eventually form a net with you in it.

Rule Number Six: If you can't have an alibi, don't have a motive, at least not an obvious one. Cops know nobody has an alibi when they are at home in bed at night, but they don't care unless they think you had a reason to kill your victim. So if you think someone might become a target, don't engage in conflict with them.

Rule Number Seven: Keep still. Once you set everything in motion, do nothing that was not part of the original plan. People who scramble to protect themselves only wind up drawing attention to the thing they want to hide.

Rule Number Eight: Avoid casting suspicion on anyone else if you can help it. It's bad karma. Unless the person is really, truly, odious.

Rule Number Nine: No Souvenirs. Souvenirs are evidence. You never know when evidence will surface. Keep your memories and nothing else.

Chapter 3

Peter rang the bell for Lia's half of a two-family at 10:00 a.m. as planned. Lia unlatched the screen door only to have it shoved open to the sound of excited whimpering. Paws landed on her thighs.

"Viola!" She knelt down for frantic puppy kisses. "Aw, sweetie, I missed you." She looked up at Peter. "Thanks for bringing her."

"Do you want me to hang onto her or should I unclip her?"

"Let her go, sure." By this time, Honey and Chewy were sniffing Viola and barking. The trio ran off to the back of the house for a canine reunion.

"Can I get you anything? I've got green tea, herbal, filtered water, or I could juice up some carrots and celery for you."

"No Pepsi? Isn't it illegal to be that healthy?"

"Cherry Coke is a deep dark secret in my life, Detective, but I only get one a month."

"That's even worse, having a disciplined vice."

"Better cuff me then. A month of jail food should rehabilitate me. Would tap water make you feel better? Or I could toss some high-fructose corn syrup into the tea for you."

"Sweet tea would be nice if you have any made up, otherwise, any kind of water it is."

Lia brought out two glasses of green tea and a squeeze bottle. "I was kidding about the corn syrup. I make simple syrup out of dehydrated cane juice because granulated sugar won't dissolve in cold liquid. This way you can make it how you like."

Peter shook his head. "I've never met anyone who actually went to this much trouble with their diet."

"I'm an artist, Detective. Artists can't afford health insurance. The cheapest and most reliable way to take care of yourself is with food. Call me up next time you can't sleep and I'll bore you right into a coma about it."

"Have a seat." Lia gestured to a mission style sofa with floral tapestry upholstery. A colorful hodgepodge of pillows cushioned the wood arms. She settled into a straight-backed oak chair rescued from a defunct elementary school. The dogs returned from their confab. Honey lay at Lia's feet and Viola jumped up on the sofa next to Peter. Chewy gave the detective a considering look.

"Careful," Lia said. "If Chewy wants petting, he'll head-bump your hand, usually the one that already has something in it. It's been known to cause accidents."

"Thanks for the warning. You seem to be doing much better than you were two days ago."

"Painting helps. It's my cure-all."

Peter nodded at a pair of canvases, one a close up of a Magnolia blossom, the other an Iris. "Those yours? They're beautiful."

"Thanks. I'm doing okay now, but it comes and goes. It also helps that I've been grieving my relationship with Luthor for a couple months now, off and on. Mostly, I'm just angry. I find it so much easier to function when I'm angry than when I'm grieving."

"I thought you just broke up?" He gave her a questioning look.

"That was the third time. The first time was in March. But he would wear me down and I'd take him back. And in my head I'd be trying to figure out a way to put more distance between us."

"That sounds pretty sad."

"It was. So what can I do for you today, Detective? You mentioned loose ends."

"There are just a few things we need to clarify. Do you mind if I record this?" Lia shook her head as Peter pulled out a small digital recorder and set it up.

"It's obvious from what you already said that Luthor was very upset Saturday. Did he have a history of suicidal moods or behaviors? Any family history of suicide that you know of?"

"Not that I saw or knew about. I always thought he was more the histrionic type. You know, swears he can't live without you, but a bit too narcissistic to ever actually do anything about it. He reminded me of a guy I knew in high school. Danny was having a fight with his girlfriend, picked up a steak knife and threatened to kill himself. Then he stabbed himself with it by accident while he was waving it around. He came to on the floor, wondering what happened. I could see Luthor doing something like that, getting caught up in his drama when he had people around and hurting himself by mistake. I can't see him getting morose and killing himself while he was alone. This was a kick in the teeth, and I don't understand it."

"Huh."

"You know what I don't get? Luthor loved an audience. He knew I'd be coming to the park. Why didn't he wait until I was there so he could stage a grand scene? Not that I wanted to be part of it."

"I don't know. What do you think?"

"I don't, Detective. It just doesn't register."

"We're trying to figure out where the gun came from. His parents said they never knew him to have anything to do with guns."

"Me neither. There are some gun nuts who come up to the park. Terry, he puts the NRA to shame and Jose has a concealed carry permit because sometimes he runs his dogs before daylight. But I never heard Luthor in any conversations with them about guns. You might want to ask them, though.

"Another thing. Luthor was fussy about his looks. I would have expected him to pick a means that wouldn't mess him up like that. He would go around wearing clothes that looked like he slept in them, but it was all very affected. It was carefully put together, and the clothes were expensive. He valued his image. I can't see him planning a suicide without considering how he would look afterwards. I know that sounds cynical, but that's the way he was."

"Did you notice the gun at the time?"

"Oh, no. I saw all the blood, and it freaked me out so much I don't remember anything until Jim found me. I don't know how I got back up to that picnic table."

"When was the last time you spoke with Luthor?"

"It was just before 1:00 a.m. I remember telling you he called me the "C" word. I hung up the phone then, and unplugged it. He might have tried my cell, but I misplaced it, so I don't know."

Peter's look sharpened at this. "How long has it been missing?"

Lia frowned. "I'm not sure. I know I used it Thursday in the studio. I usually toss it into my tote bag and it floats around in there. I might have seen it after that, but I can't say for sure. Why do you want to know about my phone?"

"It probably has nothing to do with anything, but I like to follow up on anything that's unusual."

"Oh," Lia laughed. "That's not unusual, my phone hides from me all the time."

Peter changed subjects. "I'd like to talk to some more people about Luthor's state of mind. Can you give me a list of his friends? People he would have confided in? Someone he might have talked to Saturday night?"

Lia considered. "I honestly can't think of anyone. Luthor was the sort to be highly dependent on a woman until the relationship ended, then he'd never talk to her again and he'd start with another one. She'd be the focus of all his needs. He had tons of buddies and acquaintances, I can't name them all. But they wouldn't be confidants. You'd be better checking the places he hung out. People always knew who he was."

"And where was that?"

"The dog park, of course. There were two bars he liked, the Comet and Northside Tavern. Sometimes Sidewinders coffee shop. That's about it."

"This Jose and Terry you mentioned before, how would I find them?"

"That's easy. Any morning at the park, before 8:00 a.m. Anything else you want to know?"

"Just one last thing. We know you and he were having problems. Did Luthor have cause to be upset about anything else? Any problems with work or money, any problems with other people besides yourself?"

"Luthor didn't care much about work except to get enough to scrape by. He made a big deal about struggling with his book, but I finally realized that was a pose. Did you ever see the movie *Sliding Doors*?"

"Gwenyth Paltrow?"

"That's it. The movie where she's supporting her writer boyfriend, and he's cheating on her, and she doesn't know it. Anyway, he's having a beer with his best friend and his friend asks him when the book is going to be done, and the boyfriend says something like 'I'm a writer, I'll never finish the bloody book.' Luthor was like that. When I started getting fed up with him, I kept flashing to that scene. That movie's probably the biggest reason why I never let him move in with me."

"So what was this book about?"

"It kept changing. First it was just a murder mystery, but recently he decided to introduce an alternate world scenario."

"Alternate world?"

"He went all 'Fringe.' You know, the show on Fox? Doppelgangers from another dimension? He figured the doubles could commit the perfect crime. He thought it would be an original twist on the police procedural genre."

"Ouch." Peter winced. "Money problems?"

"He was always broke, but it wasn't like he was losing money to a bookie or anything. He paid rent, bought a few beers, and that was about it."

"What about conflicts with other people?"

"Not that I know of."

"That's enough for now. I'll let you know if I need anything else. Thanks for your help." Peter packed up and started for the door. He leashed Viola and headed out to his Blazer. Lia watched him through the screen door, wondering.

~ ~ ~

The gun, would it boil down to that? She'd used an old Luger of her father's. Never registered, untraceable; it had been picked up at a gun show more than 30 years ago, before Hinkley shot Brady and changed everything. She referred to it as her "weapon of last resort." She knew how to shoot. She didn't like the idea of all the blood. But how often do you get a target ripe for a suicide scenario?

Shooting Luthor had been easy, like a fish in a barrel. She' been expecting the blow-back, so she'd worn a paper painter's jumpsuit, rubber gloves and booties, stuffed her hair under a ball cap. She'd spray painted the jumpsuit navy blue so it could pass for sweats in the dark.

She'd known what Lia would do. Luthor would call and call and finally she'd get fed up and disconnect the phone. She'd done it twice before. All she'd had to do was wait until Lia's cell started ringing, that would mean her land line was unplugged.

The cell started ringing at 1:03 a.m. He'd let it ring until he got voicemail and then called again. She ignored the phone, as if she were Lia. She assembled her gear while it continued to ring, then disconnected his current call attempt and sent him a text in Lia's terse style.

"Talk Park 2:30"

"Yes Yes Yes"

"C U There"

She'd sat a quarter mile from the dog park in the entry to MacFarlan Woods, waited for him to drive by, then followed him into the parking lot. She'd been sure to park far enough away to avoid any splatter. He was waiting in the car when she walked up, confusion on his face at seeing her. Still, he popped open the passenger side door when she knocked on the window.

She leaned in, her hand in her pocket, gun in hand.

Luthor started to speak, "What are you-"

She'd rehearsed it to get it right, whipping her hand out of her pocket, safety off, finger on the trigger, jamming the gun against his temple before he could blink. It had to be jammed against the temple, it had to be a contact wound, it had to be the right temple. It would have been easier from the driver's side, she could have just held the gun out of her pocket, below the car window, but that would have been a tip-off, being shot in the left temple. So she had to do it this way. Jam the gun against his right temple and get the shot off before he could flinch and spoil the trajectory.

The kick wasn't bad, but the splatter was more than she expected. Some flew in her face and she didn't like that. She changed into a second pair of gloves. Then the second shot, holding his hand on the gun so he would get gun shot residue on it, carefully aiming the gun through the open driver side window, sending the bullet up the hill away from the first shot. She retrieved the second shell, then began the unpleasant task of rooting through his clothes for the phone so she could delete the text messages.

When she was done, she pulled a plastic garbage bag out of her other pocket. She stripped off the jumpsuit, booties, cap and gloves and dumped them in the bag. Next she wiped off her face with a towelette she had in the pocket of the shorts she was wearing under the jumpsuit. She tied off the bag and placed it in the passenger side floorboard of her car. The whole process took five minutes, at most. A month of planning, a week of preparation, for those few seconds when she could rid the world of someone who Just Didn't Get It.

Back home, her dog sniffed her and whuffed, knowing the smell of blood and gun powder did not belong on his mistress. She'd tucked the bag in her reach-in freezer so it wouldn't tempt the dog, then taken a very long, hot shower. She cleaned the drain and sanitized it with bleach. A bit much, but you couldn't be too careful. This operation had been risky enough without leaving DNA around her bathroom.

There were enough loose ends. Lia's phone. Disposing of her clothes. Luthor's phone records. The second bullet, which might be found fifty years from now by a hobbyist with a metal detector.

Terry might be a problem. He'd seen the gun when she gave him some old camping equipment. She'd taken it along on her last camping trip and had left it with her gear by accident. That was years ago. He probably did not remember. If he did, he knew enough about guns that he might remember the make and model. One of those risks you had to deal with. Better not to do anything at all about that. She had been of the opinion that her mornings would be ever so much more peaceful without having to listen to him blast liberals and recite odes to Sarah Palin. He'd been on her list as eventually needing removal, but now was not the time. It was too soon. Too soon.

If she just held tight, everything should be okay. None of her removals had been discovered yet. As long as they continued to believe it was suicide, no one was likely to turn over any rocks looking for evidence.

Best to do nothing about Terry for now. Still, she'd come up with a plan.

~ ~ ~

Peter made plans as he and Viola walked towards his Chevy Blazer. He needed to pull Luthor's phone from his personal effects. He needed to review the contact list and call records, any text messages. That would help the time-line and maybe give him some leads. He needed to spend some time at the places Lia mentioned, talking to people. Maybe call Brent in to help with the legwork. Would it be worth it to review Luthor's manuscript? First books tended to be autobiographical. Maybe he revealed something there.

Luthor's parents were having his body transported to Buffalo. It might not hurt to ask a local to go to the funeral, see who came. He didn't think Lia was going. From his conversation with the Morriseys, he didn't think she'd be welcome.

Another visit to Luthor's apartment was in order. Somewhere in there there had to be an explanation why a man unfamiliar with guns, who was intent on dying, would shoot himself with his non-dominant hand.

Chapter 4

Desiree was the antithesis of Lia, Peter noted. The shapely bartender had a wild spray of coppery hair with lime green highlights. She had a ready smile and a Celtic trinity symbol revealed by an artful rip over her right shoulder blade. A band of bloody barb wire tattooed her left biceps. He couldn't see behind the bar to check out the rest of her outfit. He made a mental bet with himself that she wore jeans featuring butt cleavage. Peter thought the look was a bit tired and wondered about people who went overboard in their appearance. He had the thought that maybe a real artist didn't need to look like one.

He thought about Lia, long hair pulled back at the nape of her neck, plain T-shirt, serviceable khaki shorts, bare feet, short nails, no tats, piercings or jewelry. She was simplicity. Yet her paintings were anything but simple. She took the ordinary and made it lush and exotic.

Desiree put down the glass she was wiping. She glanced down the deserted bar. "Luthor was such a doll." Peter watched her face carefully. She'd become misty when he showed her Luthor's picture. It had him on alert.

"How long did you know Luthor?"

"He was a regular before I started working here last winter, but we didn't really start talking till Spring. Some time around Spring break? He was coming in a lot more often then."

Peter wondered if Luthor was more like the guy in *Sliding Doors* than Lia knew.

"How well did you know him?"

She gave him a guilty look. "Ah . . . geez. That girlfriend of his, she didn't get him, you know? Just because she can crank out pretty pictures of flowers and people lap them up, doesn't mean she understood what Luthor was going through with the book. He was writing something important, you know?"

Peter tamped down his impatience. Likely she'd gotten that opinion straight from Luthor, probably verbatim. "So you knew him pretty well. Did you see him outside the Comet?"

She looked away.

"Desiree?"

"Why do you have to know?" Her response held a touch of petulance. She pulled out a cutting board and started slicing lemons. She still didn't look at him. Peter gave her a moment.

"It's really important."

"Why is it important? He's dead! He shot himself. What else matters?" Tears gathered in her eyes. Peter knew better than to let her emotionalism distract him from the fact that she wasn't answering him.

"We need to know why, and everything matters." He kept his tone even.

She sighed heavily, giving up. "Look, there was this one night. He hung around after closing. We all have a few drinks after closing. He was wasted. I was a bit toasty. They'd broken up. We wound up necking in the parking lot and I took him home with me. He came around for a few weeks and then I found out she had her claws in him again. I couldn't deal. So I told him 'no more.' I wasn't going to be the Other Woman, and if he didn't know what he wanted, he'd have to figure it out. He tested the waters every once in a while, but after that he started to drift away. Stopped coming in so much, like that."

Peter privately thought Luthor did know what he wanted, and it wasn't to be stuck with one woman. Further questions revealed Desiree hadn't seen him for several weeks, and he hadn't called. She'd been working until closing the night he died. Whatever happened that night didn't appear to involve her.

Desiree provided names of some of the regular crowd but she didn't have numbers. He'd have to come back on a Thursday or Friday night to catch everyone. Desiree said she didn't think Luthor saw any of his drinking buddies outside the bar. Not much hope that interviewing them would reveal anything important, but it had to be covered. Maybe he could get Brent to do it.

His trip to the Northside Tavern turned up a waitress. Sharon was a black haired, dark-eyed waif who swore they'd been friends, but nothing more. According to Sharon, Lia was making him crazy, he kept trying to leave and she wouldn't let him go. He was too good for her. Lia had some mental problems and he couldn't break up with her until she was stabilized on meds.

Sharon had been out of town for her sister's wedding on Saturday night. She said she'd seen him on Wednesday, but hadn't spoken to him since.

No joy there.

By the end of the afternoon, Peter was convinced writers were being literal when they called themselves professional liars. He'd grab an early dinner and look at Luthor's phone records. Right now that looked like the only way to establish what he did Saturday night, if he did anything besides harass Lia.

~ ~ ~

Peter had never experienced anything like it. He'd brought home an Edgar Allen Poe from Dewy's Pizza. (He didn't know what garlic and olives had to do with Poe, but who really cared about a name?) And now Viola sat exactly eighteen inches away from him, her eyes tracking every bite, drool intermittently hitting the floor. After eating two slices, he closed the box, pulled out his notebook and looked up a number.

Lia answered on the third ring, thank God.

"What can I do for you, Detective?"

"I have a dog problem."

"Oh?"

"I'm trying to enjoy a nice pizza and Viola's staring at me and slobbering all over the floor."

Lia laughed.

"It's not funny. I can't eat like this."

"Well, Detective, you'll have to distract her."

"Distract her? With what? She acts like pizza is a tractor beam."

"Oh, it is, Detective, it is. You distract her with the crust, and she'll take it to some corner where nobody can take it away from her. And if you're lucky and the pizza is not too hot, you might make it half way through the next slice before she's back."

"Can't I just give her some kibble?"

"She knows the difference. She's not stupid. You'll have to share."

"And that's not bad for her?"

"It's better for her than a lot of dog foods. No chicken beaks in pizza."

"Ugh."

"Don't give her onions, chocolate, or grapes, and very little sweet stuff. She loves apples and carrots, and she especially likes avocado."

"Avocado?"

"Her favorite outside pizza and liver treats. Some people say dogs shouldn't get it, but in small amounts, it's fine."

"You know a lot about this. Sure you can't take her?" Peter hoped the desperation in his voice would engage her sympathies.

"Three dogs is very different from two. You ever try walking three dogs at the same time?"

"Um, no, and don't want to."

"Exactly. Any other Doggy Daddy advice you need?"

"Now that you mention it, I don't think she's house-broken. I take her for long walks and she does nothing, then as soon as we get home she'll find some corner and do her business."

Lia sighed. "I should have thought of that. Sorry. Viola's a complicated little girl. She was abandoned at an early age, and she gets anxious, especially in new situations. She feels especially vulnerable when she's using the bathroom. I think that comes from her Border Collie intelligence. She thinks more like a human than other dogs. You like anyone watching you in the bathroom?"

"Good point. What do I do about it?"

"She'll get over it as she feels more comfortable, but she's always had a shy bladder. Luthor would take her to the park and she'd find some nice, private bush to violate. You really have to watch her to pick up after her. You might get some disposable training pads from the pet store. She knows what they are and she'll use them. If you want, I'll teach you a little song we would sing to her on walks. It's a signal she knows."

"Are you saying she won't pee because I don't sing to her?" His incredulity was apparent.

"Viola's very special. Dogs are like people. They all have their quirks."

"Huh."

"It's a big change, having a sentient creature around all the time. They have needs and personalities, but they're still easier than children. Viola's been spayed, so she'll never come home pregnant, and while she may want to drive, she can't reach the pedals. She'll never wreck your car."

"You have a point. But you're scaring me. You sound like you think I should keep her."

"No, Detective, I think she's going to keep you. It's okay, you'll like it. Bring her up to the park sometime if you need some pointers. Dogs are easy and fun if you keep a few things in mind. Otherwise they can run your life."

"I just may do that."

~ ~ ~

Peter used the crust from his two previous slices to give him a head start on the next one. The pizza had lost much of it's heat by the time he'd gotten off the phone, but the advice had been worth it. He pulled out the Morrisey file.

The autopsy report set time of death between 2:00 a.m. and 3:00 a.m. Luthor had been shot by a nine millimeter gun that had been held against his right temple, according to stippling left on his skin. He had gun shot residue on his right hand.

All this was textbook for suicide, except for Mrs. Morrisey's insistence that her son had been left-handed. She stated he had no interest in guns and hadn't even researched them for the book he was writing. "He said he didn't need to because all the guns in his book were from an alternate universe and didn't operate like Earth guns." Her even tone over the phone made it impossible to tell how Mrs. Morrisey felt about her son's ingenuity.

These two tidbits had been enough to delay ruling on the death, and in the interest of clarification, Peter had been asked to continue investigating.

Peter read further. Toxicology was negative. Nada. Zip. Clean as a whistle. Peter frowned. Usually when a man eats a gun, he has a few drinks first. Cold steel is hard to face sober, and everything he'd learned about Luthor indicated that he was not brave or stoic, more like the type who can't look when he gets a shot. How does a guy like that pull the trigger?

None of this was impossible, but it wasn't comfortable. He might have been acting the obsessed and wounded lover but he had two other women in the wings.

He picked up the report on Luthor's phone. First was the contact list, next was the list of calls. He skipped to the last page. Saturday evening was one long list of outgoing calls to a number Peter recognized as Lia's. The last one was 12:57 a.m. Sunday morning. After 1:00 a.m., a new set of calls appeared, to Lia's cell phone. Twenty over a period of thirty minutes, again all outgoing. Peter wondered what Morriesey's other women would think about the way he was hounding the woman who "had her claws in him."

Then, at 1:35 a.m., an incoming text from Lia's cell.

Huh.

Looked like the two phones traded texts. He looked at the bottom of the report. There were no texts stored in the phone for the wee hours of Sunday morning. Whatever they had been, they were gone now.

He was going to have to buy flowers for Cynth in IT for pulling all this off the phone. In the old days, it would have taken a court order to get it from the service provider, and even if they'd had sufficient cause, they might not have bothered. Hooray for technology.

Lia said her phone was lost. Maybe it wasn't lost. Maybe it was stolen. If so, someone else used the phone to text Luthor, pretending to be Lia. Did that person set up a meet?

If Lia had lied, then she was hiding something. But what? Whatever it was, he didn't think she was at the park when he died. The woman had been in shock after finding him. If her two friends hadn't taken such good care of her, he would have called for EMTs and sent her to the Emergency Room.

He didn't like the idea that she might be more involved in this than she was saying. It didn't play with the person he'd met. But he had to admit he was a sucker for green-eyed women with long legs, and his BS meter might be malfunctioning.

Well, nuts. He'd been hoping for a tidy resolution that would allow him to find out more about Ms. Anderson with a clear conscience. He scratched Viola absently on the head. There was a silver lining to this. If Lia was feeling guilty about driving Morrisey to suicide, she could stop.

Unless she was the one who killed him.

Chapter 5

Wednesday, May 11

"Lia, darling, how *are* you?" Catherine neatly inserted herself between Lia and Jim on their bench. The hug she gave Lia had Lia's coffee tipping precariously. "How terrible for you. I wanted desperately to be here for you Sunday, but the police wouldn't let me through. I hope they told you; that young detective said he would. I made him promise. You wouldn't know, I'm sure you were in shock." She turned to Jim and touched his shoulder. "Jim, did he tell you?" Lia rolled her eyes so only Anna could see and resolved to ask her later if Catherine was batting her eyes. She swore she could hear lashes fluttering.

Lia had decided to rejoin what she called the General Population. (And didn't the mad scramble on this side of the park resemble a prison yard sometimes? A prison yard with barrel racing?) Mostly people were giving her space. Except Catherine.

"I really wanted to bring you a casserole so you wouldn't have to worry about food but I just had so much company, there was no way I could do it. I'm so sorry about Luthor, but you know, I never thought he was right for you. What an awful, awful thing for him to do. You must be devastated." She turned to Jim. "I heard you saw him, too. Was it awful?"

This time she paused in expectation of an answer.

"It was grim, Catherine. You wouldn't have wanted to see it."

"I'm sure it would have *destroyed* me to see something like that. I don't think I'd ever be the same again. I don't know what the world is coming to. I've got to run Caesar and Cleo to the groomers. She took Lia's hands in hers and pressed them. "Don't you worry, we're all going to take care of you. Caesar, Cleo, come baby cakes, it's spa day! Jim, you must walk me to my car." Jim obligingly escorted Catherine and her yapping Poms across the park.

Anna raised her eyebrows, looked sideways at Lia, and announced sotto voce, "She came, she saw, she conquered."

Marie snorted.

Bailey shook her head. "Is she always like that?"

Anna, Marie, and Lia replied in unison. "Always."

"Don't worry, Sweetie," Anna said. "She's done her good deed for the day. She can go to lunch with a clear conscience now. Tell us, what did Detective Peter want to know? Bailey, have you seen Detective Peter? He's quite handsome."

"Anna, you go for it," Lia said. "I can't deal with being fixed up right now."

"Seriously, why was he interviewing you? Surely there's no question how Luthor died?"

"Not at all. He said they were just trying to understand why, so he wanted to know who Luthor might have been talking to, if he was having problems. Aside from me breaking up with him. That sort of thing. Oh, and he called me later. He wanted some advice about Viola."

"Did he now?" Anna gave Bailey a knowing look.

"You can stop with the eyes, Anna, he's just not used to having a dog."

"So why haven't you taken her?" Marie asked.

"I don't think I could stand having her give me the 'Where's Daddy?' look. It's your fault, Bailey. You introduced me to that animal communicator. Now I know she's missing him and wondering where he is and if I took her, she might blame me for taking her away from him. I'd feel guilty every time I laid eyes on her. Besides, she likes men better."

"You know," Bailey offered, "calling Luella might not be a bad idea. She could explain it to Viola."

Marie considered. "You think a detective would go for the woo-woo stuff?"

"So maybe we don't tell him," Bailey offered. "He'd let you have visitation, wouldn't he? And Luella could ask Viola how she likes the detective."

Lia gave Bailey a look. "So devious. I never knew that about you. I'll think about it."

~ ~ ~

Thursday Night, May 12

Peter was exhausted when he finally returned home Thursday evening. His bar interviews had turned up one dead end after another. Likewise interviews at Luthor's job. While he was sure the Cincinnati Art Museum was a pit of seething passions, Morrisey, in his position as a part time art installer, appeared well out of it.

Viola wriggled and wagged as he opened the door. He knelt down to ruffle her fur and she gave him frantic kisses. Not a bad way to arrive home. He let her out the back, twisted the cap off a Beck's and sat on the stoop, watching her sniff her way around the yard.

The more he thought about it, the more it made sense that Morrisey's death had something to do with the dog park. The dog park parking lot was an excellent place for a rendezvous.

The long, narrow lot was blocked from view on two sides by trees and on the third side by the hill. You could only see the lot from the street if you looked in when you were exactly abreast of the drive. If you didn't use the lot, you might not know it was there. It was unlikely anyone but a dog park regular would think to use it. If one of Morrisey's bar pals had suggested a meet there, it would have seemed odd. The place was perfect for ambush; a public place nearly invisible from the street, buffered on three sides by hundreds of acres of forest. It might not have occurred to Morrisey that the most used six acres of Mount Airy Forest were going to be deserted and isolated at 2:00 a.m. Familiarity may have made him careless.

The dog park also appeared to be the one place where Morrisey and Lia intersected. Lia was the obvious suspect. A woman would have to be nuts if she *didn't* want to kill him after all his hounding. But that didn't feel right. While Lia was remorseful about events, he didn't feel she had the passion for Morrisey to kill him. She just seemed ground down by him and over it.

This crime had taken obsessive planning to set up and if Morrisey had not been of a small percentage of the population who preferred to use their left hand, the crime would have been labeled suicide. This type of staging took detachment. The woman he interviewed in the park was stunned, not detached.

Procedure dictated he interview her again, and hammer her about the phone. But since she or someone close to her killed Morrisey, all the interview was likely to accomplish would be to tip off Morrisey's killer that the death had been reclassified as murder.

Meanwhile, as long as he had Viola, he had the perfect excuse to hang out at the park and get a feel for who was who.

He was sure Lia would introduce him around. If she didn't, from what he saw during his one visit, Viola would draw anyone who knew her master. And he could ever so casually ask Lia if she found her cell. So far, no one knew this was a murder investigation. If he kept it that way, maybe he could catch his quarry off guard. Whoever it was.

~ ~ ~

My first removal was the hardest. Not the doing of it, I was quite glad to put an end to a life that exuded such misery that it spoiled the perfect peace of my existence. It was the pretense of grief afterwards I found hard to maintain. I decided never to remove anyone so close to me again.

But the doing was easy. My target was conveniently asleep in a hospital bed with an IV drip. So simple to use a hypodermic to load the line with potassium chloride at the end of visiting hours. When his induced heart attack occurred, I was in a very public restaurant booth with friends. That was the first time, and it was in the restaurant that I most struggled, to keep still, to stay calm, to wait for events to unfold while pretending nothing had changed. The call came, ruining a very nice Snapper Almondine. I had to abandon this treat and also forgo the Creme Brulee I had planned to order for dessert.

I learned much that night. I learned to use my own stress and tension to fuel the appearance of grief. I learned that at certain times people will forgive you if you pretend not to hear them and don't respond to them. And I learned that while it is a good thing to be visible and accounted for when the removal actually occurs, it is also good if you can be alone when receiving the news. Schooling one's voice over the telephone is much easier than also considering one's facial expression and mannerisms in a face-to-face conversation.

The first one was easy because the plan was simple and I did not over-think it. But the more removals I do, the more aware I am of how many things can go wrong, how much danger is in each step along the path once the event is in motion. As the years go by, technology is increasingly my enemy. Surveillance cameras, time stamped receipts, GPS devices, all become my enemy and must be accounted for. It becomes harder to obtain what I need to carry out these events without leaving a record. It is no longer enough to simply dispose of evidence; you have to obtain items in such a way that not a single kilobyte betrays you ever had a connection to them. I've learned to anticipate possible scenarios and obtain the necessary tools ahead of time as part of a legitimate purchase. My painter's coveralls I bought two years ago when I repainted the living room. I bought them along with two gallons of paint and other supplies, at an old store that didn't use a scanner. I paid cash. There was no camera.

I did not have Luthor in my sights then, I hadn't met him yet. But I knew someday I would need to protect myself from leaving DNA at a removal, and I put those coveralls away against that day. This gesture was perhaps my own version of a hope chest.

Chapter 6

Friday, May 13

Lia grimaced at the plans on her drawing table. Bailey leaned over, her Cleopatra haircut swinging with the motion. She indicated an area alongside the path. "I was thinking lavender along here."

"Won't it crowd the path once it gets going?" Lia asked.

"Not if we widen the path"

"Maybe. We'll have the same problem with the mint. We want it to fill in but not take over."

"That means digging out the pathway, then pounding sand into the bed. We'll need to fill in the spaces around the pavers with crushed limestone. We'll also need a plastic border along the edge to keep plants from encroaching."

"Catherine's not going to like that."

"She will once she sees the price for brick edging."

Lia nodded, "You make an excellent point, Bailey."

They continued to pore over the drawings for a free-form, paved labyrinth landscaped with herbs to provide aromatherapy. Round pavers would depict oriental symbols for peace, joy, love, harmony, abundance, and energy.

"Does she know Chinese?" Lia asked.

"Doubtful, but it's awfully fashionable, isn't it?"

"Bailey, you're such a cynic."

"I'm a pragmatist and you love me for it. That's what it takes to keep a straight face around some of these so-called arts mavens."

"This project isn't so bad, is it? Lia asked.

"No, it's better than most. We may have a tough time making a profit, though."

"Why do you say that?"

Bailey listed her reasons, "One, I can tell she's going to be insanely particular. Two, she seems obsessed with impressing her friends. Three, this seems to be a case of 'she may know art, but she sure doesn't know what she likes.' Expect materials to be rejected and for her to change her mind a few dozen times. Remind me why we took this job again?"

"Because it's an opportunity to show off our talents. And because we love pain and suffering. Want to see some tile samples?"

"Sure. So what is Dame Catherine's story, anyway?" Bailey asked.

"She's on her second husband. First husband died years ago. Current husband is a recent addition, don't know much about him. She got him through her other friends. Lia emphasized the word just enough for Bailey to notice.

"Other friends? Who are her other friends?"

"You know, the society folks she hangs with when she's not slumming at the dog park."

"Is that what she's doing?"

"Feels like it sometimes, don't you think?" Lia responded.

"I'm not sure what to think of her. The one time I had a conversation with her, she told me I had a certain poise that commanded her attention. But she wasn't sure if anyone else would look past my unfortunate features to notice."

Lia snickered. "You gotta admire a creative backhanded compliment. She really means well, though."

"I guess."

A knock interrupted their mutual eye-rolling. Lia glanced out the window. "We speak, and Madame Devil appears." Lia put on her game face and invited Catherine in.

"Lia, Darling. I'm so glad to see you working." Catherine paused to give Lia air kisses. "I was afraid that awful business with Luthor was going to derail our little project. I can't wait to see what you have for me. *Tell* me the drawings are finished. Oh, hello, Bailey."

Lia smiled her best business smile. "Just waiting for your approval."

Catherine examined the drawings. "Just marvelous. I *love* the Chinese symbols on the pavers. But I'm just wondering . . . most people won't know what they mean. Can we put the words in English around the edges, make it repeat as a border?" Behind Catherine, Bailey pointed a slender forefinger into her mouth, gagging silently.

"Not as a mosaic," Lia said, keeping a straight face with effort.

Lia could see the lure of the impossible taking hold as Catherine frowned. "Why not? I think I'd really *like* that."

"There's only room for something 1" tall. The letter shapes are too intricate for the tile, and the tile would shatter. There would be a lot of waste, and the pieces would be so small they'd be likely to pop out with the first freeze. The labor would be excessive and it would triple the cost of the pavers. And blow our timeline."

"Oh, surely you can come up with *something* more reasonable."

"We could carve something in the cement, but that means we'd have to flip the stones before they were dry and I couldn't guarantee they'd cure properly. Plus the depressions would gather dirt. And it would just be plain grey, no color"

Catherine sniffed, "Oh, I wouldn't like that at *all*."

Lia sought to redirect her. "Don't you think the words would be awfully . . . busy? Right now the indigo symbols are on a multi-colored background, for a confetti effect. It's elegant and energetic. To make the words legible, we'd have to go for a solid color background, and then your pavers would look just like something you see in every New Age store in town." Which was exactly where she got the idea, Lia thought.

"Perhaps you're right." Catherine tapped her chin with a French manicured nail.

Bailey picked up on the direction of Lia's thoughts. "I think not having the translations makes it more exclusive, don't you think? Then your guests will need to ask you what they mean. And you'll know them because this is your mantra."

Catherine brightened at this, "What a *lovely* idea. So how are the plans for the koi pond in the middle coming?"

Bailey took over here and pulled out a diagram showing a large pool with an island in the center accessed by stepping stones. In the center of the island was a circular mosaic bench that allowed you to face all directions.

Catherine sighed in pleasure at the yin yang sign gracing the top of the bench. "I wish the stepping stones in the pond could have mosaics, too."

"We need a textured surface on the stones because water will be splashing on them. With mosaics, the surface would be too slick. You could get hurt. We wouldn't want that."

Catherine pouted, "I *suppose* you're right. Can we have it finished next month? I want to throw a Solstice party and show it off."

Bailey glowered behind Catherine's back. Her long, expressive hands mimed choking Catherine.

Lia temporized. "It would be cutting it close. I'll check Jose's schedule to see when he can do the excavation. We'd really like to have time to let the pavers cure for a month for maximum strength." She ticked off a timeline. "First the plans need to be approved. Then it will take a minimum of two weeks working full time to cast the pavers, a month for curing. We can get the excavation and landscaping done while the pavers are curing. Then a two week window for installing the pavers. In order to make it work, we'd have to cut back the curing time. And any changes will set the timeline back. We may have to be creative about obtaining the herbs you want since it'll be past prime planting time. They'll just be starting so you won't have full growth until next season."

"Next season? Oh, that *won't* do. Maybe I should just put in a nice gazebo instead."

Bailey's eyes bulged. Her expression was a mixture of incredulity and outrage.

"Gazebos are so nice," Lia said, "especially the one your friend Yvonne has."

The reminder that a gazebo would not be unique in her set was enough to bring Catherine back onboard. Lia was all smiles as she escorted Catherine out the door with her copy of the contract. Once the door was closed, she slumped against it and let her mask slip.

Bailey shook her head. "Rich people."

"Jose has done some other work for her. He refers to her as the Princess from Jupiter."

"Sounds about right. But she'll have her 'perfect oasis of perfect calm,' as she calls it."

"She'll have hers, what about ours?" Lia asked.

"Mmm. What would that entail?"

"You tell me."

"Perhaps a nice little oak grove anointed with blood sacrifice? Catherine's, perhaps?"

Lia laughed. Then suddenly, tears began to trail down her face. "Shit, Bailey, I can't help thinking how much Luthor would have appreciated that."

"It's okay. You're pushing yourself too hard, maybe? No one expects you to be 100%, even if you did break up with him."

~ ~ ~

Twenty-five thousand dollars. That's what the stacks of hundreds tallied up to. The sight of the neat bundles was the last thing Peter expected when he opened the metal box in Morrisey's apartment. Apparently nobody else expected it to be there, since it had been several days since Morrisey died and the box was still there. Money usually meant drugs, but Morrisey's apartment lacked the usual signs of dealing or drug use. Blackmail? Since Morrisey was taking shape as a first class sleaze, Peter didn't doubt his scruples would've bent to allow for taking money for silence. It might explain why he was unconcerned about finishing his book or earning more money. And it provided an excellent motive for murder.

Someone had been smart. Since it was all cash, it couldn't be traced. While the existence of the money tantalized, for now it led nowhere. He'd have to file that away until they had someone in their sights. Twenty-five thousand missing from someone's bank account would be a nice nail in someone's coffin, but he'd have to get close enough to pull their bank records.

He remained convinced that the dog park was involved, but those were working and middle class people. Who up there would be dealing in that kind of cash? Suddenly he remembered his Sunday morning encounter with the histrionic society matron and her two fluff-ball dogs. What were they called? Pekinese? No, Pomeranians. She was old enough to be Morrisey's mother. What could he possibly have had on her?

He shook his head. Speculation, Dourson, pure speculation. Just as likely he was being paid by Lia's NRA buddy to run guns. Or maybe he was a killer for hire. Nah. Morrisey didn't have the stones to pull that off.

He looked around the dumpy, one-bedroom apartment furnished in College Bohemian. The hodgepodge of furniture looked to have varied antecedents, chosen for comfort and probably passed on by friends who were upgrading. He bet the Lazy Boy came from a guy whose new wife made disposal of the chair a condition of the wedding. He smiled at the thought of a pre-nuptial agreement that stated, "marriage shall be considered null and void if said recliner inhabits marital premises as of 12:01 a.m. on wedding date."

He opened Morrisey's closet. Here was where Morrisey spent his money. He may not have cared where he lived, but he cared how he looked. The array of jewel-toned shirts in high-quality fabrics reminded Peter of a peacock. Lizard skin boots kept company with Italian loafers. It seemed a bit rich for Morrisey's blood, but maybe not for the guy with 25K stashed under his Lazy Boy.

Chapter 7

Saturday, May 14

"Ho, Lia, isn't that your young man trodding the path to our little heaven?" Terry gestured towards the access road.

Bailey's bemused expression suggested she had yet to get the hang of Terry's flowery vocabulary.

"My young man?" Lia asked dubiously.

"Ah, yes, our stalwart officer of the law and his newly acquired canine companion. I'd take the lovely Viola, but then the poor lad would have no excuse to bump into our resident artist."

Lia rolled her eyes. "Have you been talking to Anna? Why don't you two go back to passing notes in math class?"

"Oh, but this *is* math class. And one plus one equals?"

Lia smiled sweetly and handed him two plastic grocery bags. "One plus one equals Jackson and Napa crouching on the other side of that picnic table as we speak. Time for latrine duty, Teddy."

Terry headed for his relieving dogs.

"Teddy?" Bailey asked. "I thought he was Terry."

"Lia's little joke," Anna responded. "She says with little round glasses he'd be a dead ringer for Teddy Roosevelt."

Bailey squinted at the sturdy figure bending over to retrieve Jackson's daily present. "Maybe, I've never seen a picture of Roosevelt from this angle."

Jim chuckled. Viola bounded up and playfully body slammed Honey. Honey took off after her. Chewy started barking. Fleece, as usual, ignored everyone.

"Okay, Little Big Mouth, enough," Lia stated firmly.

Peter walked up. "Little Big Mouth?"

"Chewbacca. It's what I call him when he annoys me."

"I thought he was Chewy?"

"His full name is Chewbacca Wonder Pup, Master of Confusion."

Peter raised his eyebrows.

"His name was supposed to be Chewy," Lia responded to the unasked question. "Marie breeds Schnauzers and she informed me that Schnauzers have too much dignity for such a silly name." She patted her thigh, rubbing Chewy's ears when he propped his front paws on her legs. "She hadn't met you yet, had she, Little Man? Anyway, I gave him a name full of consequence."

"And is Honey just Honey?"

"Oh, I couldn't elevate Chewy and leave her behind. She's Honey Bunny Sunny-Side Up."

"Huh," was Peter's only response.

"Why Detective Dourson!" Catherine announced herself as she moved in next to him. "What brings you to our tiny corner of Cincinnati?"

"Dog's gotta run." He shrugged and used the gesture to dislodge Catherine's hand from his biceps.

"So you're not here to ah - *investigate* - anyone?" Her emphasis on 'investigate' held prurient notes.

Bailey cleared her throat to stifle a laugh. Anna nudged her and Bailey nudged back.

"Should I be investigating anyone?"

"We're all as innocent as lambs and doves, Detective. I don't think you'll find any guilty consciences here," Catherine announced loftily.

"Oh, I don't know," mourned Anna. "I have to confess to murdering a hot fudge sundae last night."

"Really," said Peter gravely. "And did that murder include cannibalism?"

"Why Detective Peter, you found me out! But you can't prove a thing."

"No?"

"I ate the evidence."

Terry, having rejoined the group, guffawed. "Well turned, my lady! You definitely have more than half a wit!"

Catherine turned to Jim. "Walk with me." Jim followed her obediently, Caesar and Cleo trotting alongside.

"Was it something I said?" Peter asked.

"Oh, Detective Peter," purred Anna, "You committed the gravest of sins."

"Oh?"

"You paid attention to someone else. Terry, I see Jackson and CarGo are paying too close attention to that sweet little lab. We'd better go make sure Louise didn't bring her to the park in heat again."

Bailey pulled Kita's leash out of her back pocket. "I'm going to take Kita for a walk in the woods before I go. I'll call you later about starting Catherine's pavers. Come, Kita!"

"Well, Detective, come have a seat." Lia perched on top of a picnic table in the shade of a towering Hackberry tree. Viola raced back and jumped up next to her, presenting her winsome 'scratch my ears, please' smile.

Peter joined her on the table top. "Dogs sure seem to like you."

Lia obliged Viola. Viola turned her head to make sure Lia got the good spots. "I like them back. Viola and I are great buddies. I wish I could take her but I know my limits."

"She's okay with me for now." Honey, jealous of the attention Viola was getting, shoved her head under Peter's hand. He gave her an absent pat. He sighed. "I promised myself I wouldn't talk business, but I do have a burning question for you. Do you mind?"

"Shoot, Detective."

"Where would Luthor get a large amount of money?"

"Luthor? He didn't have any money. He talked a good game about taking me to Baja after he made a million on his book, but that was all talk."

"What if it wasn't?"

"What are you saying,?"

"I found a significant amount of cash in his apartment."

Lia's look sharpened and her voice steeled. *"How significant?"*

"Twenty-five thousand dollars."

The look of amazement on Lia's face confirmed to Peter that she knew nothing. He could see her trying to process this news. "Are you sure it was his money? I've never known him to have any."

"Whose would it have been?"

Lia frowned. "One of his buddies? It wouldn't surprise me if one of those guys was into something shady."

"What makes you say that?"

"Sometimes Luthor would say things that suggested his values were . . . ." She searched for a word, "flexible. He liked the idea of a big score. And I think he enjoyed being on the edge, where his drinking buddies were concerned. He called it research. I called it living vicariously. I could see him falling into some scheme. I don't know, I'm not sure what I'm talking about. Him having money when he was always crying poor stuns me, but on another level, it doesn't surprise me at all. Does that make any sense?"

"Huh."

"Detective, the more I talk to you, the more I wonder where my brain was when I got together with Luthor."

Peter decided a neutral response was the better part of valor. "I'm sorry to upset you."

"Don't apologize. I don't know where the money came from, but in a weird way, it makes me feel less guilty over his death."

Peter thought of other things he could tell her that might remove all her guilt. Seeing her reaction to the news that Luthor had other girlfriends would be informative. But that would violate confidentiality.

"Lia, look at me." He lifted her chin with his index finger.

Her gaze was quizzical.

"The only guilty person is the one who pulled the trigger."

"You don't think breaking up with him was its own kind of trigger?" She asked softly.

"I don't know exactly what happened with your boyfriend, but the money suggests that there was more going on with him than a break-up. I'm just not sure what."

"Will you find out?"

"I don't know. I'll do my best."

"This is a lot to take in. Do you mind if we don't talk about it anymore?"

"Sure, if I can ask just one more question."

"What do you want to ask?"

"Was Luthor left or right handed?"

"Left. Why would you want to know that?" Her confusion had Peter mentally heaving a sigh of relief. If she'd known that, she couldn't have shot Luthor because she wouldn't have made the mistake of shooting him in the right temple.

"Just filling out the profile. No big deal," he lied.

"I'm going to go throw balls for Honey. You can join me if you like. I don't feel much like talking, but if you're with me the others will stay away."

"Why is that?"

"Just their bizarre sense of humor."

She led him to an open space with a gentle downhill slope and pulled her flinger and a couple of tennis balls out of her tote. Honey bowed and barked in anticipation. Chewy returned from reconnoitering. Viola went on alert. Lia relaxed with the mindless activity. Peter sat and watched her, her fluid movements, her unguarded affection for the dogs. It was rare that he had such uncomplicated pleasure while working. Thirty minutes later she left for her studio.

Jose had left, but Terry was still there. It didn't take much for Peter to engage Terry in gun talk. He waxed poetic about his favorite rifle, what he called his "Sarah Palin Special." He expressed his preference for the Walther PPK as a personal protection weapon, and debated the merits of revolvers versus pistols for police work. When Terry was well warmed to his topic, Peter asked him who else around was a gun enthusiast.

"Aw, these guys are amateurs." He named a few names. "Jose has a concealed carry permit because he's up here before daylight lots of days."

"Why so early?"

"He's one of the few morning people who works day shift. He often needs to be done and gone before eight."

"Is it that dangerous here that he would need a gun?"

"Well, at one time, the men's room was a big gay pickup spot. We cynics think they put the dog park here to run them out, but we still occasionally get the odd hopeful. Then there was a rumor a few years back, that someone was using the corral at nights to fight pit bulls. I doubt you'll run into either at 5:30 a.m., but I guess you never know."

"You seem to know a lot about what goes on up here."

"About as much as anyone."

"We still have some things we're trying to clear up about Morrisey."

"Luthor? What about him?"

"We're still trying to figure out what he was doing with a gun. His mother swears he avoided them. Did he ever talk with you about guns?"

"Certainly."

Peter perked up.

"Tell me about this. What was the nature of those conversations."

"Conversation. Singular. He wanted to discuss a murder weapon for his book, so I reviewed the differences between pistols and revolvers, and Barettas versus Glocks and the impact of a .22 round versus a 9 millimeter on the human body, and how caliber size affects exit wounds. He got a bit green at that last part. I think that's when he came up with his 'double from another dimension scenario,' so he could just make it up as he went along."

"So where does a guy like that get a gun?"

"Good question. What kind of gun?"

"Luger 9 millimeter. It's more than thirty years old, not registered."

"Fascinating. And as untraceable as they come. Luger, huh? Not the kind of piece you'd find for sale in a bar parking lot, I'd say."

"No," Peter agreed, "Not something that old. This one was pristine. Someone cared for it. I'd say he got it at a gun show, but then it would have been registered."

"Not a family piece?"

"No, not at all. The Morriseys don't own guns."

"Curiouser and curiouser. You check old posts on Craig's list?"

"One of the guys did. Nada."

"You, my man, have a true mystery on your hands."

~ ~ ~

Keep still. That's Rule Number Seven. It's hard watching Detective Dourson talk to Terry, hard not to barge in and either derail their conversation or at least find out what they were saying. Better not. Showing my face to Terry when they might be talking about guns might jog his memory. I'm dying to know what they're saying. Is Dourson's presence as benign as he pretends? Lia looked upset when she left. They must have been talking about Luthor. I can get her to tell me about it later.

I'm going to have to come up with some story in case Terry asks me about the Luger. He only saw it for a moment. Does he remember what make it was? Terry's mind is a repository of endless depth. I need a story for what happened to it, something plausible. Let him bring it up if he must.

Or would it be better to admit I own a Luger, then be distressed that it's missing? Is it plausible that Luthor would have stolen it? What's worse? Owning the suicide weapon, or not being able to produce an old Luger when he remembers? If he remembers.

It all depends on Terry. Will he remember?

~ ~ ~

Peter was startled out of his musings by a deft touch on his arm.

"Detective, I feel so neglected," Catherine purred. "You'd rather listen to Terry's odious opinions than talk to me."

"Purely business. Tying up loose ends."

"I'm sure I can tie up a loose end as well as anyone."

"Maybe you can. How well did you know Luthor?"

"Oh, about the same as everyone else. That is, excepting Lia, of course." She gave a little laugh. "After all, he was young enough to be my son. Why do you ask?"

"We're trying to figure out where the gun came from."

"I don't think I can help you there. Are you sure you don't have any other ends I might . . . tie off?" Peter avoided rolling his eyes, barely.

"I was confused about one other thing."

"What is that, Detective?"

"Luthor seemed to dress rather well, don't you think?"

"I always did admire a well put together man."

"So where did he get the money?"

"What do you mean?"

"His clothes seemed a bit rich for his finances. Did Lia give them to him? Was that why he didn't want to break up with her?" He saw a flash of something in Catherine's eyes. Then it was gone.

"Lia?" Catherine tittered, "Have you seen the way she dresses? I can't imagine her going to the trouble of dressing a man. Can you?"

"Hmm," Peter was non-committal.

"Nothing against dear Lia, you understand, but personal appearance isn't a passion with her."

Peter took in the champagne hair, artfully cut and highlighted to match her beloved Pomeranians and wondered what Lia, with her flip flops and no-nonsense ponytail, thought of it. Catherine, on the other hand, did have a passion for personal appearance. He decided to push a bit more.

"Luthor was a real puzzle."

"How so, Detective?" Wide hazel eyes looked perhaps a bit too innocent.

"You've got a would be writer with a nothing job. He likes his beer, but that seems to be his only vice." He paused. "What's he doing with twenty-five grand in his apartment?" Did he see a jolt of fear before she looked away?

"Perhaps," her affectedly winsome smile returned, "He got it the same place Ollie North did."

"How so?"

"From his change jar."

Peter didn't get the reference. He made a mental note to ask Alma, his octo-generian neighbor.

Lia's passion might not be personal appearance, Peter mused, but Catherine was obsessive about it. None of his interviews suggested a connection between Catherine and Luthor. Still, she was the only person in Morrisey's orbit who might have 25K to spare. Was she capable of murder? She might be if blackmail was threatening her lifestyle. He didn't have anything solid yet, but at the first hint of probable cause he'd be all over her financials.

Chapter 8

Lia and Bailey eyed the stack of paver molds. It had taken the better part of a day to cut 12" circles out of 3" thick, 18" squares of foam insulation to form the sides of the molds. Each foam square would be paired with an 18" square of 1/2" plywood, which would be the bottom.

The mosaic designs would be arranged right side up on a template. A sheet of contact paper would be adhered to the tops of the tiles to hold the design in place. This would be flipped and laid on top of the plywood, and the template removed. The styrofoam form would be placed around the design, then concrete would be poured in the hole, on top of the tile. When it was unmolded, the finished paver would be turned over to show the face of the tiles.

Lia nodded at the stack of styrofoam molds. "We've got forty forms. Depending on how inspired I am, I should be able to set up the mosaics for those in one to two days. Then a day for us to pour the concrete. Those can set for two days while I lay out the next batch on the extra set of plywood squares. The trick is going to be keeping the finished concrete thoroughly wet while it cures."

"We could get some kiddie wading pools and keep them submerged."

"That would work, but they wouldn't hold enough pavers. After we pop them from the molds, we're going to wind up stacking them at least five high. We could cover them with wet burlap and plastic, spray them down every day."

"Put styrofoam shims between to protect them? Then we'd be able to spray in between the pavers."

"We'd have to be careful. Don't want the stacks falling over because the shims made them unstable."

"Good point."

Lia rolled her shoulders to get the stiffness out. "I'm so glad she went for the random confetti background, it will make it so much easier to produce a few hundred of these. And even though there are six repeating symbols, every paver will be unique."

Bailey nodded in agreement. "That's what I thought. So while you're getting this going, I'll go out to Catherine's with Jose and stake out the area for him to roto-till. After he does that, we can mark the path, the beds and the pond. He can dig out the path and lay down a bed of sand."

"Will he pound it down with that funny vibrating thing?" Lia asked.

"Funny vibrating thing? Is that a technical term or are we talking artificial appendages?" This came from Anna as she stuck her head through the doorway. "I tried to call your cell. You know your mailbox is full?"

Lia sighed. I still haven't found my phone. But I'm not looking very hard. I'm not looking forward to clearing out those messages."

"We could try calling it," Bailey offered, "but I suspect the battery would be dead by now."

Anna strolled over and perused the stacked forms. "Oooh, I see lots of pizza in someone's future. Pizza and caffeine. So is

Madame Butterfly paying a fast food surcharge for wrecking your diet?"

"I'm going to move my spare juicer in here and pick up a 15 pound bag of carrots at Whole Foods. My diet won't go totally down the toilet."

"Hear that, Bailey? Our girl not only has a juicer, she has a spare juicer. How many people do you know have spare juicers? But enough about art and food. Let's talk about sex. I ran into Catherine and Marie at the park. They tell me you were having quite the tete-a-tete with Detective Peter."

"It was nothing. More questions about Luthor."

"What more could he possibly want to know?"

"A lot, apparently. Mr. I'm-Too-Broke-To-Take-You-On-A-Real-Date had twenty-five grand stuffed in his Lazy Boy."

"No!" exclaimed Anna and Bailey in unison.

"Where on Earth did that come from?" Anna asked.

Lia's expression became troubled. "Anna, that's the sixty-four thousand dollar question. Or I should say, the twenty-five thousand dollar question. That's so impossible, my circuits are fried. I don't even begin to know where to go with that. Bailey, would you have thought Luthor had even spare change to drop in the cushions of his recliner?"

"He did always dress nice," Bailey observed.

"He said his mom sent him clothes. I never questioned it. Now I'm wondering if 'Mom' is some burly guy in Columbia with a shaved head."

"Luthor didn't travel enough to be a mule," considered Anna.

"He could have been picking up packages at the airport for someone," Lia said.

"Really, Lia, you think his Corolla would make it that far?" Anna responded.

"I don't know," Bailey frowned. "Luthor had an elastic view of the world, but drugs? I can't see it."

"I know," replied Lia, "But what can you see that isn't worse?"

"Oh, Lia," Anna apologized. "I've gone and gotten you all upset. I'm sorry."

"It's okay, it was just simmering there below the surface."

"Sweetie, we don't have all the facts. We don't know for sure what that money was doing there. It might not have even been his."

"Yeah, he could have been holding it for the big burley guy with the shaved head. Somehow it doesn't make me feel better."

"You don't suppose he got a book deal?"

"And took it in cash? And didn't tell the whole world?"

~ ~ ~

What rotten luck. Who would have thought Luthor could hang on to twenty-five dollars, much less twenty-five thousand? And that Dourson would find it? Now he's got more questions, and he'll continue digging.

So far, I have been peripheral to this investigation. This is my third investigation. I've never been a "person of interest," though this time there are more loose ends that could trip me up.

My first removal was too close to me. It was exciting being in the spotlight, though it was very exhausting and I had to keep up the pretense much longer than I cared. I became a virtual prisoner in my own home just to avoid people. But the bliss! It was worth the risk to have serenity again, with the added pay-off of an inheritance. That first removal was such an epiphany. That I could remove people who disturb me! The blights on existence that make life less than pleasant for the rest of us could be eliminated. This exhilarating truth made my self-imposed confinement both necessary and difficult. I wanted to skip down the street and sing tra-la-las. Not a good look for someone in mourning.

I spent my time in planning. Thinking how it could be done, deciding who might be next and how long I should wait. I rated the people around me. Considered their good and bad points. It really all boiled down to who was making life unpleasant and was unlikely to change

I felt like Santa Claus, making a list and checking it twice.

My second removal came a year later and I don't think anyone would have argued with my choice. He was a stupid man, misogynistic, always yelling at his kids, the dogs. Drinking beer on his porch wearing a Marlon Brando undershirt (I refuse to call them "wife-beaters") displaying an unpalatable physique. His was the only worthwhile opinion on any matter, and I'm sure if he ever apologized to his wife for anything, she'd have fallen over in a dead faint.

He was tricky, having so many people around him. My break came when one of his children complained that they never had peanut butter in the house. Dad was allergic and almost died once.

I waited until he was leaving for his annual hunting trip, then left a bag of brownies in his truck. I made them with peanut oil. He went into shock in his hunting blind and wasn't discovered until his buddies missed him hours later. I'd put the brownies in a plain white bakery bag, layered with tissue. The police figured he picked them up at some country store during his trip. There were too many miles and too many back roads to find the source. The only fingerprints on the bag were his.

There was a token investigation, centered around his wife. She was properly bewildered and was not a baker. A search of the house did not reveal chocolate or peanut oil. She received her life insurance, sold the house and moved away. This was a relief to me because she was just the sort of woman to find another just like him. And if she *didn't, her boy was getting old enough to start displaying behavior he learned at Papa's knee. Their house was soon occupied by a young couple who refinished the floors, tore out the cabinets, and exorcised the ghost of Archie Bunker, Jr.*

Removal number three was a supervisor who thought nothing of demanding that I work on the weekend and deliver reports to her home after hours. None of which was necessary. On one occasion, she was home with a cold. I brought along a bitter herbal powder. I told her it would help her symptoms and offered to fix her some in some water. She was touched by my consideration. I laced it with sleeping pills. When she passed out, I put on rubber gloves and rinsed out her glass to eliminate any residue. I wiped my fingerprints off the jar of herbs, and pressed her hand to it. Then I put it in her cabinet. I dragged her into the bathroom, removed her clothes, and ran bath water. When it was half full, I placed her in, pulled up on her ankles so that she was flat on her back under water. She never woke. I had read how it is impossible to rescue one's self from drowning when the feet are held up like this. I held her feet up for five minutes, just to be sure, then carefully repositioned her legs with bent knees, to look like she had been sitting in the bath, passed out, then just slid under. I scattered her clothes around as if she'd dropped them on the floor in a drugged stupor. On the way out the door, I dropped a few more pills on the table, picked up my report and left. I was never there.

Universally disliked as she was, I saw distress but not grief at work. Our new supervisor lacked her flash and drive. He also lacked her temper and demands. Though I did not find him engaging, he was workable and not out to prove anything. I was not the only person who appreciated his willingness to trust in staff competence and the lack of eleventh hour revisions.

It was ruled an accidental death. All evidence suggested she was alone when she died and no one looked any further.

Lia was saddened but not destroyed by Luthor's death. She would converse, even laugh at a joke. But then she would go flat.

Would grief cause her to dive into her work or leave her enervated and listless? She had a project to finish, a gorgeous serenity garden. If Luthor's death had a negative impact on her work, would it be any worse than the negative impact he was having while he was alive?

Chapter 9

Sunday, May 15

Peter felt like a heel. The birds were chirping, the early morning temperature was pleasant. Viola was enthusiastically tugging her lead as they passed through the gate to the park. And her foster-dad was using her to have a reason to spend time here so he could figure out what was going on with the morning crowd. He was using Viola to get closer to everyone, but especially to Lia. If there had not been a murder, he'd be using Viola to get closer to Lia anyway. Because there was a case, he was keeping secrets from her. Everyone who hung out at this patch of the forest was to some extent a person of interest and he had to be careful.

The motive had him stymied. It could be a jealous lover, but Luthor struck him as a man who believed in self-preservation. So far his investigation revealed a man who kept his women apart. Peter was sure Morrisey's killer had a connection to the park. Since Lia was here daily, he couldn't imagine Morrisey inviting trouble by allowing one of his girlfriends to cross paths with Lia, especially not here.

It could be the money. If only he could figure out where it came from and what it was for. Or the money could have nothing to do with it. It could be a big, fat, sexy red herring. The initial search had missed it. Could someone have planted it later to distract him? Who would have 25K to throw away like that? And how would they know he'd find it?

The four big motives for murder were money, sex, revenge, and power. Occasionally someone killed to protect their ass, but it hadn't happened on his watch. Sex or money seemed the likely motive for offing Morrisey. Maybe a CYA if the money was for blackmail. He wouldn't count revenge out, though it was last on his list. Morrisey seemed the kind of guy who avoided trouble. He might indulge in a little discrete blackmail if the victim were unlikely to retaliate. He was not a guy who tugged on Superman's cape.

Peter's musings were interrupted by a golden body slam. Honey careened off his legs as Viola chased her around him, wrapping his legs with her leash. Peter, still reeling from the hit, toppled. He looked up to see Lia's jade eyes laughing down at him, her hand extended to help him up. He took her hand, not for the assist, but for the opportunity to touch her. Her hand was long and graceful, strong and soft. He felt a jolt when they connected. Her eyes briefly flashed wariness, and he wondered if she had felt the connection as well.

"And that, Detective, is why we remove leashes inside the corral before we enter the park."

"Oh, is that the reason?"

"One of them."

"Will the others prevent me from landing on my ass?"

"They might."

"Then enlighten me. Please." He gave her a pathetic look.

"Okay." She thought for a moment. "You see the corral?"

"Yeah, I got the whole leash-corral connection."

"This is something just as important."

"Do tell."

"A corral has a gate. A gate is a portal."

"Okay," Peter replied, unsure where she was going.

"Dogs guard their space. When they are inside the park, the park becomes their space and the gate is like the front door."

"And?"

"What does a dog do when a stranger comes to the door?"

"They, umm, bark?"

"Yes, and sometimes they get aggressive."

"So dogs in the park guard the gate?"

"Sometimes they do, if they are near it. So it's best to take your dog away from the gate after you enter the park, and don't let them guard. You don't have to worry about Viola with that. But . . ."

"But?"

"If you're inside the corral, and dogs inside the park start guarding, there's a chance a fight might break out."

Peter's expression became intent. "So what can you do?"

"If a strange dog is guarding the gate and they are acting aggressively, snarling and growling, call their owner over and ask them to remove their dog from the gate. You have an advantage, you can always flip your badge out if you need to."

"That wouldn't constitute an abuse of power?"

"I'd say letting your dog be a bully is an abuse of power. You're just calling them on it."

"Okay, I can buy that. What else?"

"Don't ever bring food or treats into the park. Some dogs are food aggressive, so it can start a fight."

"Makes sense."

"Don't ever put loose treats in your pocket. I think Viola has outgrown chewing the pockets out of pants, but even if she has, your pants will always smell like treats and you're likely to get pestered. So any time you carry treats, keep them in a baggie. Of course, if you're recruiting drug dogs, that would be a way to sniff out the talent."

"Pun intended?"

"Of course. One big thing. Dogs are pack animals and they have to either lead or follow, so if you don't lead, they will decide it's their job, and they'll start behaving badly."

"How do you do that, besides with a leash?"

Lia pondered for a moment, "It's more about being consistent. Only have a few rules, but make them rules you can and will enforce every time. You can't neglect it even once. You let it go and they know it's not really a rule and they don't have to do it."

"Sounds harsh."

"Nah. It just simplifies things. I'm not saying boss her around all the time. Set basic routines around walks and meal times, and when they know what to expect, they'll start doing it automatically."

"And if I don't?"

"Say somebody is harping on you to lend them money. If you've never loaned them money, they'll give up pretty quickly. If you used to lend them money and now you're saying no, it's harder to get them to go away, right?"

"True."

"Now suppose you spend fifteen minutes saying 'no' and then they wear you down and you say, 'Well, okay, but this is the last time.'"

"Okay."

"So what happens next time?"

Peter scrunched his eyebrows and thought. "He's not going to believe me when I say no."

"Exactly!" Lia flashed a broad smile at his astute response. "Viola has a couple routines she knows, so it should be easy to get her back into a groove. But once you start with her you can't blow it off."

"So what are they?"

"When it's time to go for a walk, have her sit before you clip on her leash. And when you are done, make her sit to unclip." Lia lifted her hand, palm up, and Viola plopped on her butt. "Okay." Viola popped up. "That's the hand signal. Or you can just say, 'Sit!' in a firm voice." Viola sat back down.

"I haven't been doing that. So what do I do now if she ignores me? "

"You say 'sit' the first time and if she doesn't do it immediately, say it once more, but this time gently push her butt down. Don't keep repeating the command, then it just becomes noise. Like teachers in school who yell all the time and nobody listens to them. So what ever it is, give her one opportunity to obey, then if you need to, repeat the command and gently put her into position. And if she pops out of position, keep doing that until she stays."

"Doesn't sound too hard. So what else is she used to doing?"

"Viola's used to being told to lay down before she gets her meals, and she's not allowed to eat until she's released. You release her by saying 'okay.'" Viola got back up, this time she sauntered off, hoping to avoid more commands. "Always have her hold a command until you release her."

"That sounds a little mean."

"Dogs are different from humans. They like being led unless they're being led by someone ineffectual. Viola may give you some resistance, she may test you by trying to get up before you release her. "If you let her get away with it, pretty soon she'll be jumping all over you when it's meal time. She might start snatching food from your plate when you're eating."

"Sounds like a slippery slope."

"It is. Dogs know who's a push-over and who isn't. And their behavior will change accordingly."

"I have nephews like that."

"Exactly."

"If I make my nephews lie on the floor before I give them pizza, do you think they'll stop acting like brats?"

Lia laughed. "It's worth a try, Detective."

"So are you going to teach me Viola's pee song?"

"I don't know. That's pretty personal stuff. I don't think I know you well enough. I think you should make up your own pee song."

"Damn. Must I?" He looked at her sideways. "I think you're making the whole pee song thing up just to con me into making an ass out of myself."

She gave him a look of mock-affront and batted her eyes at him. "Would I do that? She splayed a hand on her chest for emphasis. "Moi? To an officer of the law? Surely not!"

"Well, when you put it that way."

"Besides, I don't need to humiliate you. You'll do it to yourself the first time you talk baby-talk to Viola in public."

"Oops."

"See, humiliation is already a done deal. Surrender your self-respect, Detective, it's very freeing."

Peter decided they'd talked enough about his personal humiliation. "So how long have you been coming here?"

"Ever since I got Honey, about six years ago."

"And you come up here every morning?"

"Pretty much. Except when it's pouring rain or the roads are iced up."

"And the same people are here everyday?"

"Some more than others."

"And you're friends with all of them?"

"Good friends with a few, friendly with most of the rest. You'll find all different kinds of people here, and you wind up associating with people you wouldn't know otherwise. Sometimes the only thing we have in common is dogs. We all try to get along, but if the sordid underbelly of the park were exposed, I suspect you'd find a seething cauldron of political conflict, romantic discord and social rivalry."

"And which of these are you?"

"Until last Sunday, I guess I fell in the category of romantic discord. I guess I'm still there. I feel so guilty."

"Why?"

Lia's earnest green eyes suddenly glimmered with a hint of tears. She glanced to the right, and then down. "I hate what Luthor did and I hate that he did it because I broke up with him and I especially hate that I'm relieved that at least it really is over. His funeral is next week and whatever I do, I'm the bad guy. I stay away and it's because I don't care. If I go, then how dare I show my face after what I drove him to? I thought about sending flowers, but I suspect they'd wind up in the trash."

"Have you talked to his family?"

"I called his sister on the phone and she screamed at me for five minutes straight before I figured out there was no point in staying on the line."

"I see what you mean." Peter took a deep breath. Every instinct he had said Lia was being truthful, and her glance to the right before she shared her feelings confirmed it. She was remembering, not fabricating, according to the workshop he had taken on interviewing techniques and reading kinetic cues. That, and she knew Luthor was left handed. Still, trusting her would be a risk. Would it be worth it?

"Lia, let's go sit down somewhere. I have something to tell you." Peter hoped he wasn't making a big mistake.

"Over there?" Lia pointed to an empty picnic table under a Maple tree. They climbed up on top and rested their feet on the benches.

"Why do so many people sit on top of the tables here?"

"Dunno. Maybe because if we sit on the benches we might get slammed by a racing dog, or one of the dogs will jump up on the table and get in our faces? Maybe just maintaining pack leadership? Height is dominance to dogs, so you'll see little dogs jumping up on the table so they can lord it over the Great Danes and Rotties."

"Huh." Peter noticed talking about dogs relieved some of the stress he'd seen in her. He hoped what he was going to say would eliminate some of her guilt. He also hoped she wouldn't shoot the messenger.

"So what are you being all mysterious about?"

"What I'm going to tell you has not been made public, but I think you need to know. Can I count on your discretion?"

"Hard to say, since I don't know what it is. I'll stay mum if there's no compelling reason not to."

"Fair enough. Look, Lia," He paused and Lia turned to him, searching his face. He tried to figure out how to present this. "Luthor shot himself with his right hand."

"And?"

"He's left handed."

"What's the big deal about that?"

"Have you ever held a gun?"

"No. Never."

"They can be pretty heavy. It would be awkward handling it with your non-dominant hand, even for someone who knows how to shoot."

"What are you saying?"

"We don't think he shot himself. We think it was staged to look that way."

She stared at him. Her shock was immediate and real. "There's more."

"More?" The word escaped her mouth in a high-pitched whisper. She swallowed.

"Did you know Luthor had other girlfriends?" This time she looked away. He wondered if killing the messenger was occurring to her now. He kept on, doggedly. "One young woman he saw the previous time you broke up. He attempted to keep it going after you got back together, but she wouldn't have it."

Lia gave a sad and cynical snort. "At least somebody had some class."

"The other woman he started seeing casually recently. She seemed to be more a girlfriend in waiting. It hadn't quite gone there yet."

Lia kept looking down, shaking her head. Finally, she said, "This is too much. Luthor was murdered?"

"We think so, yes."

"Why?"

"We don't know. Lia, did you ever find your cell phone?"

"No. What does that have to do with anything?"

"Because Luthor received a text from your phone shortly before he was shot. We have to find it."

~ ~ ~

Anna and Jim watched from the other side of the park as Honey jumped up on the table and licked Lia's cheek. Lia turned her head into Honey's neck and wrapped her arms about her, taking comfort in the silky warmth.

"What do you suppose he's saying to her that has her so upset?"

Nadine walked up. "Lia looks really unhappy. Should we interrupt?"

"I think she needs space right now," Jim replied, "She knows we're here."

Catherine walked up and took Jim's arm. "Hello, Anna, I just love your sweatshirt. You look so . . . *relaxed.*" Anna ground her teeth. Catherine turned her attention to the pair under the tree. "Honestly," she said, nodding at Peter and Lia, "Why is he distressing her like that? She's in the middle of a big project. She doesn't need this."

Anna rolled her eyes. "Catherine, you're all heart."

"You'd feel the same way if it was your garden that might be late and your party that might be ruined," Catherine pouted.

"No, I wouldn't. And he didn't need to do much of anything. Lia's got a brave face, but our girl's been hurting. It's only been a week since Luthor died."

"Now, ladies, we all care about Lia," Jim said

"Of course," responded Catherine. Anna just narrowed her eyes until Catherine blinked and looked away.

~ ~ ~

Peter wondered if he'd dropped too many bombs at once. It took all his patience to sit quietly while Lia communed with Honey. Viola jumped up on the bench and rested her head on Lia's knee. Chewy bounced up on the table and shoved his head under Lia's hand. She scratched his ears absently while she brooded.

Eventually she sat up and turned around. "You dumped all this on me and I can't share it with anyone."

"Not for a little while, unless you have a priest or a therapist."

"I suppose I could talk to the dogs about it," she smiled weakly.

"Yes," he smiled wryly back. "You can talk to Honey and Chewy. I'm so sorry. I didn't want to tell you like this."

"Why did you? Why did you tell me?"

"I didn't want you to feel guilty about Luthor anymore."

"Oh. Is the way I'm feeling now supposed to be better?"

"Maybe not. But at least it's based on reality. It was unfair for you to keep blaming yourself."

"So you keep coming here, what, because I'm some kind of suspect?" Lia accused.

"Not to me. I should be treating you like a suspect but that feels totally wrong to me. I think his death has a connection to the park. I think the answer is here somehow, but if it weren't, I think I'd be coming up here anyway because I like you."

"I'm not ready for this. I'm not ready for any of it."

"I know you aren't. You could help me though."

"How?"

"You know the players. You can give me background information. "

"You really think somebody here did this? I can't believe it."

"It has to be someone you know. They had to have access to you to take your phone. And they'd have to have been to the park to know how secluded this lot really is, even though it's right on the street. They'd have to know you had a fight and that you were likely to unplug the phone."

"This keeps getting better and better."

"I'm really sorry. Do you see why it's so important that you not talk about this until I say it's okay?"

"I've got to tell them something. Everyone who's here knows you said something that upset me and everyone who's not here will know by tomorrow," Lia pointed out.

Peter pondered. "How about if you just tell them about the girlfriends? Will that work?"

She nodded. "Sure. I guess so."

"I'll need to interview you more formally, and record it. Later today, if possible. I can come by your place."

"How about the studio? It'll be easier for me to talk if I'm moving my hands."

"Will it be private?"

"Sure. Bailey's going to be out with Jose today, tearing up Catherine's yard. She won't be helping me."

"Can I give you a lift? This might not be a good time for you to drive."

"We walked up today. I think I need the walk home."

He watched her walk over to her friends, looked on as Marie and Bailey came out of the woods and joined them, saw Anna put an arm around her and stroll with her to the corral and down to the parking lot. He wished it could be him comforting her. But it couldn't. At least she had someone.

~ ~ ~

Keep still. This was getting increasingly harder. That scene at the park, what was that about? Surely it had to be more than Luthor's bimbo girlfriends. How could Lia not have known? And why was Dourson still pursuing this? She'd been over it again and again. She'd made no mistakes. Yes, the cash confused things and that was too bad. But people with money and extra girlfriends could still kill themselves.

She thought of a scene from the movie, Lord of the Rings, *when the hobbits are hiding under the road as the Nazgul pass over. Worms and centipedes and every creepy thing imaginable are coming out of the earth to get away from the ringwraiths and they're crawling all over the hobbits, and the hobbits can't move a muscle or they'll be discovered.*

Keep. Still.

Chapter 10

Sunday, May 15, continued

Lia pulled out her template for "peace." Catherine's labyrinth called for fifty pavers featuring the symbol. Maybe if she dedicated today to "peace," some of it might rub off on her. She laid the circle on her work table and opened the box of midnight blue tile cut in random shapes. She got out her nippers and goggles and pulled up a stool. Arranging the tiles to fill the shape of the symbol absorbed her. When she was done, she filled in the background with random pieces of rose, saffron, and yellow. She gave the final design a once over, tweaking the tile shapes so that there was room for the concrete in between. Then she cut a one foot square of clear contact paper and laid this on top, carefully rubbing it on the tile so it would hold the pieces in place while the paver was cast.

After she did this, she took a mold base and lined it up on top of the contact paper, so that the template, tile, and base made a sort of sandwich. She carefully flipped the stack so the mold base was on the bottom and the tiles were upside-down. She replaced the template with a styrofoam ring and set the completed mold on a shelf.

"One down, thirty-nine to go."

When Peter arrived, she was working on her sixth mosaic layout. "You look like you're feeling better."

"Much. Making art is so centering. Can I get you something? Water? Sweet tea? I remember you like it."

"Tea would be great."

She pulled a jug of tea out of her studio fridge and poured two glasses. She dragged another stool over to the table. "I hope this is okay, I don't have regular chairs here."

"This is fine. What are you working on?"

Lia described the garden she and Bailey were creating for Catherine and showed him the mosaics she'd already set up. "We're using jewel tone colors, like aura colors"

"What do aura colors look like?"

"Clear and intense, like a rainbow or prism, but more variety. In addition to Roy G Biv . . . ."

"Roy G Biv?"

"It's an acronym. You know, red, orange, yellow, green, blue indigo and violet. It's the order of colors in the rainbow."

"Never heard that one before."

"Anyway, along with Roy, you can also have, say, turquoise or peach and blues from royal to cerulean, spring greens, forest greens. Browns, black, grays, and muddy colors, too, if you're unhealthy. Anyway, that's what Bailey's aura-reading friend says, I wouldn't know. So the background of each symbol is meant to evoke aura energy without being obvious about it. Catherine wanted to do a repeating rainbow theme, you know one red paver, one orange, one yellow, all through the labyrinth, but Bailey and I talked her out of it."

"How did you do that?" Peter asked. "She seems like a determined sort of woman."

"Bailey's so funny. She'll say, 'Oh, that's such a great idea! And then she mentions some tacky place where she's seen it before and Catherine can't change her mind fast enough. I caught on, so now I do it, too. Say, should we be wasting your time talking about this?"

"It's not a waste at all. Anything that helps me understand the park crowd better is helpful. If I record this, will you be self-conscious?"

"Dunno. You can try."

He set his digital recorder on the table and turned it on. "You were telling me about Catherine."

"You want more of this stuff?"

"Sure. So she sounds like she's very concerned with her image."

"Pretty much. She's the sort who won't leave the house without make-up on."

"And this project, the aromatherapy labyrinth and koi pond, that's a big undertaking. So what's that about besides wanting to be the coolest kid on the block?"

"She said she wanted an 'island of serenity' and she's seen labyrinths and aromatherapy gardens. She wanted to put it all together." Lia gave him an earnest look. "I feel kind of sorry for her."

"Why is that?"

"When you're that socially competitive, when you're that focussed on material things, well, I don't think you can like yourself all that much because just you by yourself is not enough."

"So you're wise, as well as talented?"

Lia snorted. "If you say so."

"When did Catherine decide she wanted the garden?"

"Not long after she started coming to the park. Three months ago? She found out I was an artist and started having all kinds of ideas. I thought it was just talk, so many people like her dangle their money in front of you and never come through. Like talking about doing a big commission means you're going to suck up to them. But somehow the idea caught hold and she got serious, even if she does argue about every nickel. I might have to give Luthor credit for selling her on the commission. He kept talking about what a romantic setting it would be for her. I don't know if you've noticed, but she really eats up up male attention."

"I noticed. So was she interested in Luthor?"

"How could she not be? He used to play up to her. It was like a game to him. Or at least he said it was like a game to him. Now I'm not sure anything he told me was true." She moodily pushed some tiles around.

Peter wasn't sure either. There wasn't anything he could say to that, so he changed the subject. "How about your partner, Bailey?"

"We're not partners, except on this one project. She's a woo-woo queen."

"Woo-woo queen?"

"She hasn't suggested we hold a seance for Luthor, not yet, but she's into just about every other New Age thing. Chakras, aromatherapy, herbs, acupuncture, energy healing, animal communicators, astrology . . . . She's at least tried it. She's a great landscaper. She only started coming to the park recently. I've known her for years through library events."

"You sound a bit skeptical of her inclinations."

"I really don't know much about all of it. She says she's seen auras a few times. Maybe if I saw an aura or two I might be more interested. But it's a huge market, and she can talk the language. She's interested in the healing potential of plants, both in the herbs and in what she calls 'High Vibration Gardening.'"

"What's 'High Vibration Gardening'?"

"It's a new concept she came up with, using specific plants to create an environment that encourages certain mental and emotional states. I get lost when she talks about it. She says it's like the music woo-woo people who claim listening to Mozart aligns chakras, but with plants."

"Huh."

"Anyway, when we're done with Catherine's garden, we're going to take pictures and shop it around on the internet and at New Age fairs and see if we can drum up some business."

"Why gardens? I thought you had a good thing going with the paintings."

"I do, but this is fun because it's physical in a way that painting isn't. And it will be like a painting you can walk through. When I get Catherine's bench done, it'll be a painting you can sit on." She grinned at the thought.

Peter smiled back. "Sounds nice."

"It will be. Catherine bought the house next door to her last year and tore it down, said it was an eyesore and she didn't want to look at it anymore. You know the old neighborhoods around here, showcases next to dumps. If you ask me, she was just as happy to get rid of the neighbors. She didn't like their 'breeding.' Anyway, she's been dying to do something showy with the lot, and this is it."

"So what's someone like her doing hanging out at a dog park?"

"Good question. She doesn't seem like the type, does she?"

"Not to me."

Lia crinkled her eyebrows as she considered this. "Well, some of us are arty, and she likes that. When I'm being cynical, I think she comes because her husband won't come anywhere near the park. Too much poop for Leo. She can flirt as much as she wants and none of it will get back to her society friends. When I'm not being cynical, I think it's a relief to be around people who don't care how she's dressed or how much money she has. But that could just be me. If I was around her crowd all the time, I'd go bat-shit crazy and I'd be rolling in the mud for relief."

This created an interesting visual for Peter, which he chose not to share. "So, how does Jose fit in?"

"He's doing the parts that require machinery. Right now he and Bailey are roto-tilling."

"What's his story?"

Lia smiled. "Jose is Jose. Though, now that I think of it, he's not really Jose."

"How so?"

"Jose is a nickname his family gave him when he was a baby. He says when he turned two, the thing he said most was 'no way.' So they started calling him Jose, for No Way Jose. He won't tell us his real name. He does say that he's Italian. He's your basic good-guy, who works with his hands and loves his wife. He's a maintenance supervisor. He knows how to fix most things and he does minor construction jobs on the side. He's always helping somebody with something, and if a dog fight breaks out, he's first to jump in to stop it. He probably played football in high school, but I don't know for sure."

"So how does he get along with everyone?"

"As far as I know, he gets along great with everyone. He gets frustrated sometimes when he's running a crew. Some of the young guys can be punks, and there was a guy who was stealing materials from a job last year. That just comes with the territory when you're a boss. Oh, yeah, he was really pissed at one of his neighbors for neglecting his dog, so he stole the dog."

"Really?" Peter's eyebrows shot up.

"The guy was such a jerk. He said, 'If you want to feed him so bad, go ahead and keep him.' Mostly, he's a teddy-bear. Have you seen his bumper sticker?"

"No, why?"

"It says, 'Mean People Suck.'"

Peter laughed. "I take it that's his outlook on life?"

"Something like that." Lia pulled a pre-cut square of contact paper off of a pile and peeled the back off. She expertly laid it on the tile design. Peter watched as she went through the process of setting up the mold and put it on a shelf with the others.

"And how many times are you going to do that?"

"Three hundred. But not all today." She lay the template back on the table, sat back and stretched. "I have some finished pavers if you want to see the end result." She pulled the plastic sheeting off the stacks of pavers in the corner.

"Pretty. What's the symbol mean?"

"This one is 'joy.' Today I'm working on 'peace.' I thought I could use it today."

"So what about Anna and Jim? Are they part of this grand enterprise, too?"

"You'd think this was a dog park project, wouldn't you? Anna, she's a good friend of mine. I couldn't have her working on Catherine's garden, she'd be making jokes about putting land-mines under the pavers. It would totally skew the whole 'higher vibration' thing."

"Bad blood there?"

"Well, sort of. Have you ever noticed how Viola gets jealous?"

"Jealous?"

"Sure. You pet another dog and she's right there, squeezing in?"

Peter thought back. "Never realized that was jealousy."

"Oh, sure. Catherine does it, and she does it a lot with Jim, and it tends to ruin whatever we might have been talking about when she butted in. She doesn't just join the group, she cuts him out of the herd, so to speak."

"So what does Jim do?"

"Nothing, really. Jim was married for more than thirty years before his wife died a few years back. He says he always does what women tell him to do. He seems to think that will keep him out of trouble. I figure it only works if only one woman is telling you what to do."

"And what does Anna do?" Peter asked.

"Make catty remarks, mostly. I think her deal is that eventually people will catch on to Catherine's games and if they don't, they deserve her. Bailey says that's because Anna's a Scorpio."

"What does being a Scorpio have to do with it?"

"Bailey says Scorpios love to sit back and watch people hang themselves."

"And what's Anna's story?"

"Let's see. Never married."

"Any guys around?"

"Just Jim, in a really casual way, just friends. She seems to like being single. She and Luthor didn't like each other much. I guess because she was right about him and maybe he knew he couldn't charm or con her . . . like he conned me," she finished softly.

"What did she think about Luthor?"

"Luthor liked to get milage out of being a writer and Anna was never impressed by him. She kept saying 'when is he going to buy you a meal that doesn't come on a bun?' and 'There's no romance in going dutch.' For all her advice, I don't think she's ever dated much. She lived with her dad for years. She took care of him until he died, then a few years later she sold the house and moved to Cincinnati. That was ten years ago."

"Where'd she come from?"

"Somewhere around Pittsburgh. If it was me, I'd have traded in the hills for some flat land."

"Does she work?"

"Sure, she used to be an administrative assistant at this high-powered ad agency. Now she works part time for a private foundation that funds projects in children's education. Surely this isn't relevant, all this stuff? I feel like I'm boring you with nonsense."

Peter reassured her. "People are never boring, and I never know what might be relevant. Every detail helps to create a picture."

"But don't you do background checks, that sort of thing?"

"Sure, but that's places and dates. You're giving me the heart. VICAP hasn't popped any 'murder disguised as suicide' cases. So I'm going to have to solve this the old-fashioned way."

"VICAP? Isn't that the violent crime data-base? You think the guy who shot Luthor did it before?" Her eyes widened as she set her nippers down.

"I have to say it was slickly done. If Luthor's killer had realized he was left-handed and gun-shy, we would have taken it as suicide and we wouldn't be looking at it at all."

"So we could be talking about a serial killer?" Shock warred with disbelief on her face.

"You see the problem, don't you?" Peter asked earnestly. "If this is his first mistake, there's no telling how many times he's gotten away with it before. Donald Harvey killed dozens before anyone realized patients were being murdered. Right now, we don't have a clear-cut motive. It could have been the money. If Luthor was blackmailing someone, maybe it was because he knew they killed someone."

"Blackmailing a murderer doesn't sound too smart."

"No, it doesn't does it? "

"Detective Dourson, you are just one surprise after another. I don't know what to say. How are you going to find this person if they're so slick?"

"It's a good question. Look at people who know the park, know you and Luthor had a fight and had access to your purse that day to steal your phone."

"Why did they have to steal my phone that day?"

"Because they timed this with your fight. The fight had to happen first."

"Oh."

"Then think about personalities and look at past histories, see if anyone has a pattern of deaths around them, but that's going to be hard to find."

"How come?"

"With Donald Harvey, all the deaths happened at nursing homes where he worked. There was an increase in the death rate at every job he had. Once somebody started looking, the pattern was there. If Luthor's case is one of a series of multiple deaths, the connections could be difficult to spot. We have no idea what kind of pattern to look for. It won't be anything as obvious as multiple dog park gun-shot suicides. The only connection I have is you."

"Me?"

"And your phone. Has anyone else died around you in the past few years?"

"My grandfather died about five years ago in Georgia. Cancer. Nothing weird about it, and no connection here."

Peter sighed. It couldn't be that easy. "Whoever took your phone might return it. If it turns up, don't touch it, call me immediately."

"Why?"

"It might have trace evidence. I doubt it, but we could get lucky. Anyone else at the dog park with deaths around them?"

"Most of the morning crowd at the park are over forty, some are retired or nearly there. By the time you're that age, people have died around you. I'm still having a hard time accepting that someone killed Luthor. But a serial killer? At the dog park? That's mental! So are you looking at single males between the ages of thirty and fifty? Isn't' that the profile? There's plenty of those at the park."

"Doesn't have to be a guy. Women kill, too, and they have more subtlety. Whoever it is, isn't impulsive and is very organized and detail oriented. I suspect they're very intelligent.

Lia sighed. "So we can't blame this on the homeless guy who's been sleeping in the picnic shelter."

"Afraid not. Unless you let him get near your bag."

"Are you kidding?"

"Didn't think so. Look, I know you don't like the idea of saying any of your friends could be a murderer. But serial killers are often really good at acting normal, so you might not be able to tell. How about this. Who in that group couldn't have done it?"

"Well, Jose."

"Why not?"

"When he gets mad, he puts it right out there. He's too straightforward about everything. If he got mad at you, he'd punch you in the nose, then he'd forget about it. And I don't think he could keep a secret to save his life. His wife Carla says she's got to put a cap on his poker money because he's always losing." She thought for a moment, "And he's too good-natured to keep his mad on long enough to plan something like this."

"Good. Who else?"

"Jim's retired. He was an engineer, so he's smart and organized. He does this 'Mr. Cranky Pants' routine, but it's mostly for entertainment value."

"So how does that work?"

"If you tell him he should have done something a different way, or if Terry dumps too much Republican propaganda on him, he gets blustery, all out of proportion. But he's not nearly as irritated as he seems. At heart, he's the guy you go to if you want to talk about something that's bugging you. He's also the most consistently spiritual person I know. He's Catholic and makes a real effort to live according to his faith. He doesn't make noise about it, he's not preaching or showing off. You wouldn't know that about him unless you got to know him well, so I can't believe it's an act."

"Okay." Peter filed that away for further consideration. It wouldn't be the first time piety hid a murderous nature.

"Catherine . . ." Lia twisted her mouth and nipped a corner off a violet tile while she considered the dog park diva. "Anyone who dyes their hair to match their dogs has to be detail oriented. And she's narcissistic enough to not care much about other people. I don't know if she's smart enough."

"How so?"

"Well, she's really obvious in her little games at the dog park, and I think she believes she's being subtle. Wouldn't your serial killer have a more accurate perception of how people are responding to them, if they're going to fool everyone?"

"Maybe, but not necessarily."

"Besides, she doesn't get her hands dirty. If she shoplifted as a teen-ager, I'm sure she paid the maid's kid to do it for her. She pretty much wallows in not knowing how to do anything practical. I'd think a killer like you're describing would need to be self-reliant and resourceful. Catherine is neither."

"Huh."

"Aside from that, I think underneath everything, Catherine really wants to be liked. I think a lot of her posturing comes from insecurity. I know that doesn't quite sound narcissistic, but that's Catherine. I don't think you off people when you're looking for attention."

"You sure you're really an artist and not a shrink?"

"Geezlepete. This is giving me a headache. I can't think anymore right now. Can we continue this some other time?" She set down her nippers and gave Peter an imploring look.

"Sure. Lia, I know this is hard, and finding the person could get ugly and even dangerous. I really appreciate your help. I know it's hard to keep all this inside, too. Do you have any friends across the country, someone who has no connection with Cincinnati?"

"Yeah, I've got my sister in Texas."

"If you need to talk to someone besides me, talk to them. Please don't share anything about this being murder with anyone here, no matter how much you trust them."

"Okay."

"Seriously. That person might be innocent, but you don't know who they'll tell. I mean it."

"I said okay," Lia huffed.

"Look, will you feel weird if I come hang at the park tomorrow? It would be good for me to see more of your crew, but not if it's going to make you nervous."

"Let me think about it. Can I call you in the morning?"

Lia showed Peter out. When she returned to her work table, it all seemed so pointless. She shoved the template aside, planted her elbows on the table and put her head in her hands. She stayed that way a long time.

Chapter 11

Monday, May 16

Sometimes being a cop sucked, Peter mused while he drove down Westwood Northern Boulevard. Viola was in the back seat, panting in his left ear while she caught the breeze coming in the window. All he ever wanted to do was serve and protect. But what happens when doing just that hurts someone? Especially if, for once, he wanted to get closer to that someone. Would Lia always associate him with Luthor? Too bad he didn't have Brent as his full-time partner, he would have made Brent break the news to Lia so she wouldn't associate him with Luthor's betrayal, or with the news that one of her friends was probably a murderer. And if she took his advice and called her sister, well, Sis was probably urging her to leave town . . . permanently.

He thought back to the message he found on his cell when he got out of the shower. She hadn't sounded too disappointed to be talking to voicemail. She said she'd be gone from the park by 8:30, if he wouldn't mind waiting until then to run Viola. Meanwhile, she would call if she thought of anything that might help him. Did she just want some space, or was this a full blown brush-off?

He knew she wouldn't be there, but he still scanned the parking lot for her car as he pulled in. Well, he had background checks an phone records to review, he could give her a day or two. No more than that. Lia was closest to the center of this thing and the first of Detective Dourson's Axioms for Investigators was find the center and stick to it.

Anna pulled up as he was letting Viola out of the back seat. "Why, Detective Peter," she smiled, "You're becoming quite the regular. Does this mean you plan to hang onto Luthor's orphan child?"

"Hello, Anna. Jury's still out. But she's growing on me. It would help if she learned how to vacuum. Or if she could at least shed in a designated shedding zone."

"Designated shedding zone. That'd be a cute trick. You talk to Jim and he'll tell you that her purpose is to teach you all about unconditional love, and if she were perfect, you couldn't love her unconditionally."

"Say again?"

"She has to be flawed. If she didn't inconvenience you in some way, then you'd never have to decide to love her anyway." She opened the back of her SUV and CarGo jumped out. CarGo stood perfectly still while Anna clipped on his leash.

"I'll give that some thought. So Jim is a philosopher, is he?"

"Our very own Will Rogers. I imagine you're too young to remember him."

"I think I had a layover in an airport named after him."

"That would be Oklahoma City."

At the top of the drive, they met Terry exiting the corral. "Greetings, Detective. How goes your investigation?"

"As they say in cheap paperbacks, we are pursuing all leads."

"Ah. And are there any leads?"

"That would be the question, wouldn't it?"

"Did you ever figure out where that gun came from?"

"Still looking. You got any ideas?"

"Not yet, my good man."

"You still got my card?"

"Indeed I do. And the search for the elusive source of Luthor's firearm continues."

Peter shook his head as Terry, Napa, and Jackson headed down the hill. "Does he always talk like that?"

"Like a British country squire? Always, though I've never caught him saying 'pip, pip' or 'tally-ho,' thank goodness."

Peter meandered the park, chatting with the group he privately thought of as "the usual suspects." Anna introduced him to several others. Everyone was interested in Luthor's suicide. All volunteered whether they had witnessed Lia's argument with Luthor, or been in the park at all that day. Nadine charmed him with her sincere interest in his accent and Kentucky upbringing, as well as her appreciation of Appalachian culture. He found himself telling her all about his great-grandmother's quilts and his grandfather's wood carvings. Marie put him on the spot, asking what the people were supposed to do with Pit Bull complaints. The dogs were illegal inside city limits, but there were no provisions for enforcement. While he was trying to figure a reasonable answer for her, she changed the subject, and asked if he styled himself after fictional homicide detective Joe Morelli or Lucas Davenport, or was he a Virgil Flowers? She wiggled her eyebrows flirtatiously at that last name. At this point a newcomer named Charlie told Marie to stop tormenting him. Charlie made a hobby of rehabbing classic cars. Peter spent several minutes hearing about Charlie's projects and debating the merits of Lincolns versus Caddys.

Viola raced up with a ratty tennis ball she'd found, so he took her to the back of the park where he could throw it for her while observing the crowd from a distance. They all seemed so normal. But that was the point, wasn't it? To be a wolf in sheep's clothing? It boiled down to two things: who had access to Lia's bag on Saturday, and who fit his profile. He wondered about Terry. Some killers like to insert themselves into investigations. Was that the source of his interest in the gun? Did Marie's mercurial temperament hide secret taunts? Did Charlie's relaxed, 'good old boy' demeanor mask a shrewd nature? Peter sighed as he leashed Viola and headed back to his car. Perhaps a few hours reviewing the file would give him some ideas.

~ ~ ~

It had been nagging at him ever since he spoke with Detective Dourson. He knew he'd seen an old Luger somewhere, sometime. Not recently. Now he thought he had it. She'd still be at the park. He could call her cell. He picked up the phone and dialed.

"Hey, this is Terry. I was just wondering something. You know that old gun of your dad's? . . . What kind of gun was it? . . . Really? You're certain? I could have sworn it was a Luger. Have you seen it lately? . . . How long has your nephew had it? . . . Because Luthor killed himself with a Luger and I've been trying to figure out where he got it. If you had a Walther, then it couldn't have been yours . . . I agree, it's mystifying, where he came up with it."

~ ~ ~

Lia looked at the stack of molds she had set up so far that day. She'd decided to work on 'truth' pavers, since truth was causing her so many problems right now. Realizing that she hadn't known the truth about Luthor, wondering what the truth was about her friends. Could one of them have killed him? Why? Luthor was self-centered, but he wasn't deliberately cruel. He wasn't particularly moral, but he wasn't the sort to mess with people, either. Who could he have stirred up enough to make them want to kill him? If this was a serial killer, if it was like in the movies, the motive could be obscure. Maybe it was the color of his hair, or he said the wrong thing at the wrong time. She knew she'd never get over this until the truth came out.

Jason was in his studio, and he had a phone. Maybe he'd let her use it to call Detective Dourson. If he brought her Dewy's for lunch, she'd talk to him.

~ ~ ~

Peter sat, frustrated, at his desk. His attempts to track down Lia's cell phone had failed. It could be the killer had been smart enough to remove the battery and SIM card. It could be smashed to pieces, lying in a ditch. Chances of finding it intact with incriminating prints on it were nil. Unless the Tooth Fairy decided to deliver it to him. He visualized Dwayne Johnson in a tutu delivering the phone on a satin pillow. Then he imagined Dwayne Johnson in a tutu interrogating suspects, thwacking them with a fairy wand. He shook his head at this bit of foolishness, then turned to the rising stack of paper Morrisey's case was accumulating.

He didn't mind reviewing files. It gave him a chance to step back and get perspective. In addition to his notes from his interview with Lia yesterday, he had more phone records from Morrisey.

It would be tedious work, matching up the numbers with names. Hopefully, most of the numbers were already identified on the contact list or the previous set of phone records. This proved to be true as Peter worked backwards in time. Most calls were to Lia. More calls to her than from her, he noticed. Some were to Sharon, the waitress at Northside Tavern. Sharon wasn't on Luthor's contact list. Peter had to look her number up in the reverse directory. Desiree wasn't, either. He wondered why and decided Luthor was covering his tracks in case Lia got into his phone. Would she do that? She didn't seem the type.

In Sharon's case there were an equal number of calls going each way. Peter suspected Morrisey's would-be girlfriend had been deliberately not calling him any more times than he called her, so as to not seem needy. The occasional calls to buddies held no surprises. Likewise the calls to Desiree. Then, about three months back, a new number appeared. A quick scan of the rest of the record showed it popping up frequently, more incoming than outgoing, several times a week. Peter turned to his computer to run a search on the number when his phone rang.

~ ~ ~

Terry set the ladder carefully, using wood blocks under the right foot for leveling. He leaned it precisely against the eaves. He was getting too old to be climbing up on the roof, but it was an easy job and not worth waiting for his sons to come over. A little Black Jack in the right places should hold the flashing around the dormer windows for several more years.

While he worked, his mind drifted back to his last phone call. He never forgot a gun and he could have sworn hers was a Luger. The gun he remembered was larger and angular. Walthers were designed not to bulge under a jacket. He'd forgotten to ask where her nephew lived. Could he have known Luthor? But if the gun was a Walther, it was a moot point. The arguments were circular, leading nowhere. Was it worth calling Dourson? He'd make the call. Right after he got down.

Terry tested the top rung of the ladder like he always did, to make sure it was still secure. Then as he started down, something shifted. He was twenty feet up when one of the supporting blocks popped out. The ladder twisted slowly as it pulled over to the right, overbalanced, and then toppled. Terry had just a moment to appreciate his mistake and impending death before he cracked his head on the flagstone steps and lay still.

~ ~ ~

"I admit it," Lia confessed as she took a healthy bite from a hot slice loaded with garlic cloves, then set it back on a paper plate. She leaned her elbows on her work bench and sighed with satisfaction. "I'm a sucker for dogs and pizza. If a dog could make pizza, I'd marry him. I'd get legal advice from that lady in Europe who married her favorite dolphin. Maybe we'd run away to Europe, elope.

Peter kept a straight face. "And what if this pizza-baking dog is a girl?"

"You think after I've crossed species, that gender is going to be an issue?" She raised an eyebrow as she looked at him.

"So what if a guy makes really great home made-pizza, say he has a wood-burning oven in his back yard. Would he have to crawl around on all fours to get your attention?"

"With the year I've been having, it wouldn't hurt."

"I guess I can see that."

Peter briefly considered the impact this would have on his joints and winced. "You know, I had this mistaken impression that you weren't a high-maintenance woman."

"I'm really not. I guess I'm put out with your gender. I'm thinking of going on a man-diet. What are they calling it? Something silly . . . a manbatical? I could join a nunnery." Lia wondered at her remarks to the detective. Had she been struck by the imp of the perverse? For some reason she seemed to be warning him off. He was a nice guy and obviously interested. Why would she want to push him away?

Peter pointed at the partially completed template sitting on her table. "Didn't you say you were working on 'truth' today?"

Lia sighed. "Truth is, I want to run away from anything that reminds me of Luthor's death. But I can't. I made a list."

"Oh?"

"It's the people at the park when I had the fight with Luthor, everyone I remember. It's over there." She gestured to the corner of the long work table. Peter scanned the page:

Terry
Jim
Anna
Catherine
Bailey*
Nadine
Marie
Jose
Charlie

"Why does Bailey have an asterisk?"

"I didn't see her at the park, but we had dinner later. She was trying to get my mind off the fight with Luthor. It didn't work very well."

"Hmm. So which of these people had access to your tote bag and your phone?"

"I left my bag on one of the tables while I threw balls for the dogs, and I chatted with everyone on the list. All of them, I guess. Look, I don't believe any of these people hurt anyone, but I know you have to go through a process. So as an exercise, I'll walk you through them."

Peter reviewed the list. "We already talked about Jim, Catherine, and Jose. Who's next?"

"Bailey, She's intelligent. She's also organized, but not excessively so."

"Okay, so why couldn't she have done it?"

"You might think this is dumb."

"Try me."

"She's a woo-woo queen. She believes in reincarnation and karma. There's that Wicca saying about how whatever you put out comes back to you threefold. I think Bailey would believe that hurting someone would wind up hurting her more than them, in an eternal, karma sort of way."

"Payback with interest, then?"

"Exactly. Whatever reason she'd have for killing someone, she'd have a better reason not to."

"I wish more people thought that way."

"There's something else about Bailey."

"Oh?"

"She doesn't tell people, you have to promise to keep this private."

"It won't come out unless it pertains to the investigation."

"I guess I'm okay with that. Look, she's a good friend of mine. One of the reasons she's so into the New Age stuff is because she has some problems and spirituality helps her sort it out."

"What kind of problems?"

"She's bi-polar. She was diagnosed years ago. She's on medication and she's stable. You'd never guess unless she told you. I don't think it means anything to your investigation, but you said you wanted to know about the players. I appreciate you keeping this confidential."

"Thanks for telling me."

Lia sighed. "Okay, moving on. Terry, I'm having a hard time with. He lives with his girlfriend, Donna. I don't know what happened to his wife. He's smart enough; Mensa smart, does trivia contests. He qualified for Jeopardy at one time. He volunteers for a lot of groups, so I'd see him as organized. And he's not impulsive, except maybe verbally. I have a hard time knowing what's going on in his head, he's always quick with a joke and you never know what he's actually thinking or feeling. He's really friendly, but then he'll toss off stuff like 'Gun control is getting all your shots in the ten ring,' or 'The only good Liberal is a dead Liberal,' and not consider how many Democrats he's talking to. Or maybe he knows and doesn't care."

"But?"

She looked up from the template she was filling in. "Aren't serial killers supposed to be child arsonists, bed-wetters, animal torturers? You aren't going to find any animal torturers at the dog park."

Peter grimaced. "The movies make it look so easy. It's never that simple. What you're doing is tremendously helpful. Can we keep going?"

"Yeah, sure."

"I noticed you haven't mentioned Anna yet."

"Okay. Anna's smart, but not in a show-offy kind of way. Terry will overwhelm you with all this trivia you don't know enough about to ever call him on it. Anna's more people smart."

"So why couldn't she have done it, besides being your very close friend?"

"I can't imagine her getting excited enough about anything to want to kill somebody. If she doesn't like someone, she'll make some awful and funny remark about them and let it go. It's not like she stuffs it, you can usually feel it when someone's angry and pretending they're not. She's not into drama. She figures what goes around, comes around, and people usually wind up getting what they deserve without her help. It's why I like hanging with her, she's pretty low-key and easy to be around."

"Okay. How about Charlie?"

"I'd count him right out," she laughed.

"Why's that?"

"His cars are his life. If he was the murdering sort, I'd say Charlie would go after the punk kids who keep breaking into his garage."

"So that leaves Marie and Nadine."

"They're both intelligent. Marie's got to be organized because she's a technical writer, she writes instructional manuals. Her sense of humor is really twisted. She's a bit rebellious, she likes to push the dress code at the corporations she works for. But she's so small. I think it would be hard to kill someone if you're small."

"Guns are great equalizers."

"I still can't see her caring enough about Luthor or anything he did to bother with him."

"Why not?"

"Well, she's gay. Men just aren't on her radar, mostly."

"Oh."

"She used to joke with me about swinging her way, and Luthor would say it was fine with him as long as he could watch. But they were both just trying to out-stupid each other. She's been in a committed relationship for a long time. She can be inscrutably Asian and insulting at the same time. I don't think she believed Luthor was the sharpest tool in the shed, but she didn't have a problem with him."

"And Nadine?"

"She's really sweet." Lia tilted her head and worked her mouth while she thought. "She's got ten grandkids. It's hard to imagine her plotting murder in between taking her grandkids to the mall and baking cookies."

"I see what you mean."

"So where does that leave us?"

"Good question." Peter closed his notebook and turned off the recorder. "Right now it leaves me back at the office reviewing paperwork and you here in the studio making pretty pavers."

Lia scowled at her template. "I hoped talking to you would help me sort this out in my head, but so far it's not really working. Some 'truth.'"

"Give it time."

~ ~ ~

Anna and Lia sat on either side of Terry's girlfriend, Donna. Bitter coffee dregs in disposable cups littered a formica side table. The waiting room clock was silent, and had not appeared to move the last five times Lia looked at it. Bailey sat on a turquoise vinyl institutional couch opposite, Jim next to her. Lia stared dully at the cracks in the aging upholstery.

"When did you find him?" Bailey asked.

Donna twisted a tissue into a rope, set it aside, picked up a styrofoam cup. "It was about one. I'd been making lunch while he worked on the roof, and when he didn't come in, I went to let him know it was almost ready. He was on the side steps, all broken up and bleeding. If he wasn't already in the hospital, I'd kick him. I've been after him for years to get ladder levelers. He said it was a waste of a hundred bucks. I'm going to waste *him* when he comes out of this . . . *if* he comes out of it." Tears rolled down her face. One dripped off her chin, landing in the cold cup of coffee she held.

"Do they know the full extent of the damage?" This from Jim.

"They'll have to remove his spleen and maybe one of his kidneys. He cracked his skull. They don't know yet how bad the head injury is. Both legs are broken. He was unconscious when I found him. He might be in a coma. They say when he comes around, even if he doesn't have any other brain damage, he'll probably have some memory loss."

"It's weird," Bailey interjected. "He called me this morning while I was still at the park. He wanted to know about my dad's old gun. He thought it might have been the gun Luthor had, but it's the wrong make. Terry was looking for a Luger. My dad had a Walther PPK and always joked about his 'James Bond' gun. And besides, I gave it away ages ago. Did he tell you about that?"

Donna smiled wryly. "You know Terry with a puzzle, he just doesn't let go. I swear that man's life mission is to find Jimmy Hoffa. He's been muttering about seeing the gun somewhere before, but he hadn't told me he thought it was yours."

Just then, Terry's sons, Joe and Robert, returned from the cafeteria. "We brought you some tapioca, Donna. Didn't think you'd be up to much else. Has there been any news?" She shook her head, grimaced, took the pudding, looked at it, then put it aside.

"I'm not ready for food yet, my stomach is still turning itself inside out. But I know I'll have to eat something before too long." She thought of the cold tomato soup and stale sandwiches on her kitchen counter. "I missed lunch. Terry's going to be so mad. I made Rueben sandwiches, and those are his favorite. I don't make them often because the sauerkraut smells up the house. If he pulls out of this, I'll make them every day, every meal, until he begs me to stop."

~ ~ ~

I hated doing that to Terry. Well, not really. His rabid right-wing political opinions are not what I want to listen to first thing in the morning, no matter how cheerful he is about it. I had no qualms about removing him, but I've never had to remove someone to protect myself, or with so little planning. If I'm honest, it was exciting. Once I realized he was remembering the gun, there was no chance I could derail him. I could only remove him.

I've never removed anyone with no preparation before, but I had a window of opportunity and I had to take it or miss out on my best chance to make it look accidental. It was the simplest plan I've ever executed. All I had to do was move one of the blocks he used to level his ladder so that only an edge was supporting the downhill side. That way, the ladder appeared stable long enough for Terry to trust his full weight on it, then his movement caused the ladder to shake and the block shifted, causing the ladder to fall.

It was a brilliant plan, appearing full blown in my head when Terry announced his intention to reseal his flashing. The main difficulty was executing in daylight and not being seen. Fortunately, most of the folks in his neighborhood work days. It was no trouble to wait in the car until I heard the aluminum ladder bumping the side of the house, and the sound of Terry climbing up. I gave it another fifteen minutes, then slipped through the neighbor's yard to Terry's property. I had to avoid the kitchen windows in case Donna looked out.

After all that, it took seconds to lean against the side of the ladder to take pressure off the blocks, then slide the top block over. My heart was pounding in my ears. I had to restrain myself from squealing my tires when I left.

The only problem was, it didn't work. Maybe it worked well enough. Important to wait, keep still. For the first time I'd broken one of my rules. Had it been necessary? I've never been threatened like that before. If Terry had told Dourson about the gun he'd seen, could I have bluffed it out? Produced another old gun? Suddenly realized my gun was, 'Oh, my goodness! Lost? Maybe stolen? Could that have been my gun? How horrifying!'

Now that I've had time to reflect upon it, perhaps that might have been the best tactic, But the tension had been unbearable. Any attention on me might turn over some very ugly rocks, if anyone looked at the right records with a suspicious eye. And, let's face it, I won't miss the right wing diatribes.

What's done is done. So far, everyone believes it was an accident. And that's exactly what they should believe.

Oh, God, what a rush.

Chapter 12

Tuesday, May 17

Was this it? Peter stared at the number. He'd highlighted all occurrences in the past year. The calls came, four, five, six times a week, always during business hours. Never at night. Never on weekends. They stopped abruptly three months ago. Right when Catherine bought her Pomeranians and started coming to the park. Could this be the answer to everything? Was it the source of the 25K? He'd thought blackmail, and maybe there was an element of that. But it was smelling more like gigolo, and maybe a bit of stalking by Mrs. Robinson. Could the ditzy society lady have done it after all?

~ ~ ~

Wednesday, May 18

"I can't believe Terry fell like that, he's always so careful," Bailey mournfully told her coffee.

Lia faced a morose crowd. "How is he? Does anyone know?"

"Last I heard, he's in a coma, and they think that's best for now, it'll give his brain a chance to heal. They were working on bringing the swelling inside his skull down," Jim informed the group. "I think Donna spent the night at the hospital. Joe and Robert tried to talk her into going home, but she wasn't having any of it."

"Poor Donna," Nadine mourned. "I'm so glad the boys are there to help her."

"It's so strange. Barely a week since Luthor, it's like the park is cursed," Bailey lamented.

"Oh, Pish!" Catherine breezed up, "No such thing as curses. Why all the long faces?"

Anna gave her a *look*. "Our dear friend Terry is in a coma because he fell off a ladder yesterday. And I'm sure Donna can use all the support we can give her."

"Aren't Joe and Robert falling all over themselves to take care of her? I'm not one for making casseroles, but let me know if you decide to send a card. Does anyone know if Jose is coming today? I was wondering when he's going to start laying out the path for my garden. Do you know, Bailey?"

"I believe he's over at Terry's checking to see if there was any damage to the gutters when he fell, and to take care of the ladder."

"I hope you're not going to let this little incident interfere with your deadline. I've got a party planned and everything has to be ready."

Lia had enough. "Don't you worry, Catherine. I'm starting on a new series of stones today."

"Really?" Catherine brightened. "Which ones?"

"Charity."

"Charity?" Catherine looked perplexed. "That's not part of my meditation mantra."

"Oh, it isn't, is it? My bad."

"Well, I'm glad to hear things are moving along. Caesar! Cleo! Mommy needs to go!"

As she turned away, Anna gave Lia a knowing look and waved her hand over her head.

"Oh, Anna, surely you don't think that went over her head?" Lia exclaimed in a parody of surprise.

Bailey made a kitty paw with her hand and clawed the air. "Mrowl," she deadpanned.

Marie shook her head and laughed. "You girls are so mean."

Anna gave her best innocent look. "Who, us?"

Bailey said, "You know Lia, that's not a bad idea. We should swap out some of those symbols. 'Charity' would be a good start, or 'Benevolence.' I'm wondering if it might have a subliminal effect on her. Masaru Emoto says that water responds to all language, and our bodies are 70% water, so maybe it'll impact her. I bet we can get paid before she finds out. What do you think?"

"I'd say make them all 'Gratitude' except if one of her society friends embarrassed her by pointing it out, she'd sue us. And she can afford better lawyers. I don't think 'your honor, we were just trying to make the world a better place' will fly as a defense, do you?"

"Good point," Anna interjected. "Can we just tape a 'Kick Me' sign to her back instead?"

"You've got to stop," Marie gasped, "You're killing me here."

Nadine tsked and gave an exasperated sigh.

Charlie shook his head with an odd little smile.

"Poor Charlie," purred Anna, "You just don't know what to do with women of intelligence, do you?"

"You all frighten me, you really do."

"Why, that's the nicest thing you've said all day."

"Well, gosh, Anna," interjected Marie, "It's 8:00. I think it's just about the *only* thing he's said all day."

"True, true."

~ ~ ~

Peter wanted to be pissed, but he only managed to be resigned. He wanted Catherine Laroux's bank records. His captain said he didn't have enough. "You have someone at her house calling him. That number doesn't have her fingerprints on it. It could have been the maid. It could have been her husband. Sure, it makes a pretty package, but you can't tie her to the gun or the cell phone, you can't put her at the scene (Peter's response that you couldn't put anyone at a parking lot at 2:30 a.m. went unappreciated) and we can't get warrants and court orders on a whim. We're not Homeland Security here, we actually believe in Civil Rights." Captain Roller's parting shot, "And Lethal Weapon 2 is not the video version of our procedural manual," had not made him feel any more empowered.

He'd have to do it the hard way, bring her in and sweat her. Or would it be better to interview her at home? Perhaps he'd grab Brent Davis and show up at her house. Pull the old, "We can do it here or downtown" routine. Brent was blond, handsome, buff, and totally impervious to women. He tended to fluster them with his Atlanta drawl while being immune to their charms and manipulations. With a woman like Catherine he would be a big asset.

He wanted to surprise her when her husband was not around. She was an active lady. Her one daily habit was a morning trip to the park with Caesar and Cleo. No matter what the rest of the day held, he was sure it would include a wardrobe change before she went about her business. If he hurried, they could catch her this morning.

Catherine was trotting down her front steps in an eye watering hot pink, lime green, and orange yoga outfit when Peter and Brent drove up. Peter pulled the unmarked into her drive and parked behind her car, just to be obnoxious. She hadn't recognized him yet. Brent got out first. Peter watched her eyebrows rise appreciatively as her head canted in a flirtatious tilt.

'Game on,' he thought.

"Mrs. Laroux," he called as he exited the car.

"Why, Detective Dourson, whatever can I do for you fine young men? Did you stop by to see Lia's masterpiece in progress?"

Peter eyed the torn up lot and thought it looked like a big pile of dirt, not exactly suitable for framing. He declined to comment. "I'm afraid this is all business, Mrs. Laroux."

"You sound so very serious. As you can see, I'm heading out right now. I'd be glad to help you if I wasn't on my way to class. You'll have to move your car."

"Mrs. Laroux, I'm Officer Davis," Brent said. "It's important that we interview you. We can do it here or at District Five. I know you want to be cooperative."

"What could possibly be so important that it can't wait until later?" Her sweet tone had Peter wondering if she had Southern Belles in her family tree.

"Murder, Mrs. Laroux," Brent shared apologetically.

"What are you talking about? Whose murder?"

"Luthor Morrisey's."

Peter eyed her carefully. She appeared surprised but not overly disturbed. He wondered if botox was interfering with her facial expressions.

"I thought Luthor shot himself."

Peter joined this delicate battle of wills. "We have reason to believe otherwise."

"Detective Dourson," her voice, still sugary, had steel beneath it. "I've told you everything I know."

"Actually, you haven't. Here on the front lawn? Inside? Or at the station?"

"Inside," she snapped, losing her coquetry. She led them to her living room. "Please sit." Her tone was ironic, bordering on derisive. A young Hispanic woman was dusting. "Rita!" Her voice was now razor sharp. "I'm sure you have shopping to do." Experienced in her mistress' moods, Rita left without comment.

Catherine eyed them once she had seated herself. "What is so important that you had to invade my home and disrupt my day?"

Ah, Peter thought, she's gone on the offensive. "Mrs. Laroux, you surely understand that when facts surface which contradict what we've been told, it's vital to seek clarification as soon as possible."

"How do you know Luthor was murdered?"

Again on the offensive, Peter noted. "Just a moment, Mrs. Laroux, I need to record this conversation. This protects all of us from misunderstandings."

She watched him with slitted eyes and tight lips. Caesar and Cleo padded in and silently sat where they could observe the detectives, looking like a pair of baleful dolls from a horror movie. 'Creepy,' Peter thought.

Once the recorder was set up, Catherine demanded again, "How is Luthor's death murder?"

"We're not at liberty to say, Ma'am," Brent responded.

"Call me Mrs. Laroux if you must, but do not call me Ma'am!" Catherine snapped.

"No, Ma'am," Brent replied, no irony intended. Peter caught the laugh in his throat before it could erupt.

"And what does all this have to do with me?"

"As you can imagine, we are now going over all our interviews. When I spoke with you before, you stated your contact with Luthor Morrisey was limited to the park and that you had met him there and did not know him very well."

She lifted one eyebrow, giving him a disdainful look, no doubt honed by years of intimidating underlings. "And?"

"His phone records suggest otherwise."

"Do tell." She attempted boredom here, but Peter could see a hint of fear around the edges.

Brent took over here. "Please explain, Mrs. Laroux, why you called Luthor Morrisey several times a week, up until three months ago."

"That," her mien remained icy, "should be obvious."

"We'd like to hear your explanation, for the record."

"We had an affair."

"How long did this affair last?"

"Two years, give or take."

"When did it end?"

"You know when. Valentine's Day. When the calls stopped."

"What happened on Valentine's Day?"

"He went away with Lia. Some little B & B, Ravenwood, I think."

"And?"

"He didn't take my call. He'd gotten serious about Lia. He wasn't entertaining anymore, so I moved on."

"Really?" Peter's voice held a deliberate note of disbelief.

Catherine narrowed her eyes, drilling Peter with a haughty look. "Really." The single word was as dry as the Mojave.

"How did you meet him?" Brent continued.

"He works . . . worked . . . at the art museum, installing exhibitions. I would run into him there."

"How often did you meet?"

"Why on Earth would you need to know that? It's been over a long time. That's all you need to know."

"Mrs. Laroux," Brent, eternally patient, continued, "perhaps you would like a lawyer who could explain to you what we need to know and what the . . . *definition* . . . of cooperation is?" He drew out the word and his Southern drawl intensified, somehow managing to be supremely polite and simultaneously insulting.

"Like Hell." She glared. "Bridge club."

"Bridge club?" Peter repeated.

"I met Luthor at that dump of his on bridge club days. My husband just assumed I was having cocktails with the girls afterwards. We met two, three times a month. Is that what you wanted to know?" The tilt of her head mocked. Him? Herself? Peter didn't know.

"Were you in the habit of giving him gifts, Mrs. Laroux?"

"Perhaps one or two. What does it matter?"

"The man's closet doesn't fit his income."

"Surely you don't think I wanted him with me dressed like an under-employed writer? I bought him a few things to wear. I enjoy dressing a man properly."

"Did you give him money, Mrs. Laroux?"

"Now, why would I do that?"

"Mrs. Laroux, right now we're just interviewing. However, if we're not satisfied with the results, we can always get a court order for your bank records. If we were to get those records, would we find cash withdrawals totaling twenty-five thousand dollars?"

She sat, stony.

"Mrs. Laroux?" Peter inquired again.

Nothing.

"Of course, if we serve that court order, it's likely your husband will hear about it and be brought into this investigation," Peter continued.

"I can't believe it."

"Can't believe what, Mrs. Laroux?" Brent asked.

"He said he needed the money for gambling debts. I thought I was saving him from being beaten with a tire iron. And he just stashed it away. Lia said you'd found it in his apartment. I don't think he spent any of it. I didn't know he wanted me for his retirement fund."

"Did all the money come from you?" Brent asked.

"I don't know. I didn't keep track, did I? It's so insulting."

"What's insulting?" Peter asked.

Stony silence again.

"Mrs. Laroux?" Brent prodded.

Nothing.

"Tell us about your dogs," Peter said.

"You think Caesar and Cleo did it?" The sarcastic quirk of her lips had a nasty edge.

"We just find it curious," Brent commented. "You . . . ah . . . *dump* . . . Morrisey and then buy a couple dogs and start . . . *frequenting* . . . the park where Luthor and his girlfriend are sure to be." Brent's accent, Peter thought, was a weapon, investing myriad implications in a single word in a way that could not be defended against.

"I needed new interests, Officer. Dogs love you and they're there when you need them. I can't say that about too many people, can you?"

"The dog park? Do Pomeranians require that much exercise?"

"They require socialization. The other dog parks are in West Chester and out by Lunken Airport. Or down in Covington. I'm not driving thirty miles just to socialize my dogs. Luthor did not concern me. We were friendly at the park, that's it. You act as if I were stalking him."

"*Weren't* you?" Brent's voice was soft as butter and sliced like a Ginsu knife.

"No, I was not." Her eyes flashed hot, angry. Peter could swear he heard a low growl, but that could have been Caesar. Or Cleo.

"Go ahead and ask me, Gentlemen."

"Ask you what?"

"I'm presuming you think I had something to do with poor Luthor's death. I can't imagine you'll leave here without asking me where I was that Saturday night. So ask me, then leave."

"All right, Mrs. Laroux, where were you the night Luthor Morrisey died?" Peter inquired.

"Right here in bed. Just like I told you last time we talked."

"You mean the same day you told me Luthor pulled twenty-five grand out of his change jar?"

"Was there a question in there, Detective Dourson, or are you just bent on humiliating me?"

"Mrs. Laroux?"

She quirked an eyebrow.

"Don't leave town." It was a poor excuse for a parting shot, but Peter could see from her expression that it had scored well enough.

Once outside, he turned to Brent. "You did really well in there. What do you think?"

"I think I wouldn't want my johnson anywhere near those sharp little teeth of hers."

Peter choked. "How do you think it went?"

"She was all sugar and spice until you called her on lying to you. I don't think calling her 'Mrs. Laroux' all the time helped any either."

Peter grinned. "No, it didn't." He looked back at the house. Catherine was glaring at them from the porch.

"We'd better leave before she has the car towed. Don't know if she'll be in the mood for yoga after her little chat with us."

"I suspect not, Brent."

Peter and Brent were silent as they got into the unmarked and pulled out. Once they turned the corner, Brent said, "I wonder if she dumped him after he started blocking her calls."

"Interesting thought. Why do you think he was blocking her calls?"

"Because there's not one call after February 13th, according to the records you showed me. Before that, there's up to ten calls in one week. I figure she thought he was her personal toy and after she'd bought and paid for him, how dare he cut her off. I bet she tracked him down after he blocked her calls on Valentine's Day. She doesn't strike me as the sort of woman who likes taking second place to another woman. She'd want her boy toy to jump every time she snapped her fingers."

"I think we're in agreement," Peter said. "Perhaps her demands became too much for Morrisey. They tell me it's an unwritten rule for cheaters that you don't talk to your partner in illicit lust on holidays. Still, you gotta wonder why Morrisey would ditch the goose that laid the golden egg."

"And why the goose bought herself a pair of furry bookends, if it wasn't to allow her to intrude on his life with Lia. That business about needing to go to the park to socialize her dogs is bogus. She lives in Clifton, all she needs to do is walk them down the street. Dogs everywhere here. I think she was too insulted to just fade away."

"True," Peter agreed. "The question is, was she insulted enough to put a bullet in his head and a gun in his hand?" He spotted a UDF convenience store and pulled in. They grabbed coffee and Krispy Kremes and headed back for the car.

"Why are we being so stereotypical?" Brent queried.

"It makes the public feel more secure," Peter deadpanned. He selected a cake doughnut, held the bag for Brent. Took a sip of his coffee and watched the traffic on Clifton Avenue heading up to the University. "So what do you think of Mrs. Laroux? Did she do it?"

"She's narcissistic enough to not let it go when her boy toy dumped her. She's got to be fairest of them all so if something destroyed that little fantasy, I can see her deciding he has to go. But I don't know if I see her faking a suicide."

"How come?"

"Three reasons. First, narcissists don't think they'll ever get caught, so I don't think she'd go to so much trouble to cover it up. She would have left finger prints on the shells, something."

"Okay."

"Second, while I can see her shooting him, I think she'd be in a real pique. I think she'd act her anger out. I don't think she'd stop at one bullet in the skull. I think she'd go for the family jewels, tattoo 'asshole' on his chest in bullet holes, something."

"And number three?"

"This is the weakest point. I know a lot of society ladies have learned to put on whatever face they need to suit the occasion, but I do think, under the botox, she was genuinely thunder-struck."

"Good arguments. So when are you going to go for the detective exam?"

Brent grinned. "Next month."

"Good luck with that."

"By the way, I read Morrisey's manuscript last night."

"What did you think?"

"I'm still trying to figure out why a doppelganger from another dimension would care what anyone does in our little corner of the universe, and what use he would have for Earth currency."

Chapter 13

Lia pulled up the tarp and surveyed the stacks of finished pavers. Bailey peered under the plastic cover. "How are they doing?"

"We need to spray them down again, but they're doing fine. We're ahead of schedule, so we might be able to finish a bit sooner than expected."

"Let's not tell Catherine. If we say anything to her, she'll forget 'might' and hold us to a new deadline no matter what the contract says."

"True." Lia made a moue.

"Are you ready to pour the next batch?"

"I've got the tarps on the floor. You start mixing the topping concrete and I'll lay out and oil the first ten molds."

They worked efficiently. Once the topping was ready, they split it into two batches and used a combination of pouring, scraping with a spatula, and tapping the base of the molds to force the concrete down between the tiles. It was slow work.

Bailey finished her smaller batch and began adding water to the regular concrete that would form the body of the pavers. While she did this, Lia laid precut eleven inch circles of chicken wire into the molds for extra strength. Bailey scooped the new mix into the molds. Lia pulled the edge of a planed one-by-two across the top in a zigzag motion to level out the mix, scraping the excess over the rim into a gallon milk container with the top cut off. Bailey followed behind Lia, tapping the sides of the molds with a paint stirrer to cause trapped air to rise to the top. Lia started the row over again, using a trowel to 'finish' the concrete with strokes that resembled icing a cake. This step caused aggregate to sink below the surface.

While she did this, Bailey dumped the rest of the concrete onto a slag pile outside, dropped the tools into a five gallon pickle bucket half-full of water, and hosed out the tub she'd used to mix the concrete.

"Ready for a break?" Lia held out a Starbucks Frappuccino ice-cream bar for Bailey, then ducked back into her dorm fridge to get another for herself.

"Do I get a Frappuccino bar after every set we pour?"

"Hah. We'd both blow up like Jabba the Hutt on Prozac if we ate that much ice cream."

"Let's see, three hundred pavers, divided by ten, that's thirty bars apiece. Surely we could handle that?" Bailey asked.

"Next time we bid a job, I'll have to add in the cost of ice cream and a week at a spa to work it off." Lia nibbled delicately at the chocolate as she relaxed on a stool.

"Make the spa in Costa Rica."

"Sure, Bailey, whatever you want. I assume you also want a pair of hunky masseurs to feed you grapes after your yoga sessions?"

"Can they be twins?"

"Absolutely."

"If only."

"Hey, we keep doing this, we might get to build our own little spa down in Costa Rica."

"You can forget the spa. Just send the twin masseurs." Bailey deposited her ice cream stick in the trash. "Any word on Terry yet?"

"He's stable. Right now they feel the coma is helping him heal. If it goes on too long, they'll re-evaluate his condition."

"That's so rotten. Weird, I got that call from him at the park, and a few hours later he's in the hospital. Can you believe he thought Luthor got that gun from me?"

"Where'd he get that idea?" Lia asked.

"Not sure. I don't recall ever showing Dad's gun to him. I might have told him about it, since he's such a gun nut. Terry seemed to think he'd laid eyes on an old Luger somewhere around here. Where do you suppose it was?"

"No telling. As many gun shows as he goes to, I'm surprised he can keep straight what he's seen where. But then, his brain is a repository for trivia."

"So, is Donna taking care of Jackson and Nappa?"

"Jose is helping out. He's been tossing them in the van and taking them to the park. Donna's a wreck, she spends every minute she can at the hospital."

"By the way, what's been happening with the delightful Detective McDreamy? I've seen him at the park a couple of times recently, but never when you're there. I could have sworn he liked you."

"I dunno. He's talked to me about Luthor a few times. It's upsetting, all the stuff Luthor was into. And me not knowing anything about it."

"Is finding out where the gun came from so important?"

Lia wanted so badly to share with Bailey the last revelation, that Luthor had been murdered, that the gun was critical. But Detective Dourson hadn't given her the go-ahead. She ignored the question. "I feel a bit guilty, he called as I was getting ready to come here and I didn't pick up. Didn't want to deal with him. He's been really decent, and he is attractive. You know I like long, lean men with puppy-dog eyes. But every time I talk to him, I find out something even more horrible than the last time we spoke."

"That would tend to put a girl off. Poor guy. So instead of shooting the messenger, can I have him? I promise to treat him badly."

Lia smirked. "I'll have to think about it."

~ ~ ~

Despite Brent's observations, Catherine was still the only true person of interest in the Morrisey case. But without a connection to the gun or the cell phone, there was no case. He hadn't shared his theory of a serial killer with Captain Roller. Brent had cautioned him on that point, and he was right. Inventing unsolved homicides out of yet unidentified deaths was not a good career move. With nothing but instinct to support his theory, he'd be asking for trouble. He wondered how Terry was doing. Jim told him about Terry's call to Bailey right before his accident. He wished he could pick his brain. It might be the break he was needing.

Catherine was avoiding him at the park. Apparently she hadn't told anyone about his visit with her Wednesday. Probably didn't want anyone finding out about her and Luthor, and figured keeping her mouth shut about the whole thing would keep a lid on it. Better for him for the time being. She kept staring at him with murderous looks from across the park. Jim asked him what he'd done to make her angry. He'd just shrugged. Lia wasn't taking his calls. He guessed he couldn't blame her. At least he had Viola, and he could count on one female to like him.

~ ~ ~

My favorite removal was a convenience store clerk. I bought a cup of decaf at this store every single day, for years. Then a snotty little blond began working Saturdays, and there was never any decaf when I went for my paper. She always said she would make a pot if I was willing to wait, which I wasn't. This went on for several months until one day I went in and found a full pot of freshly made decaf. Ken, the manager was at the register. I expressed to him my delight that it was available. He said, "I keep telling them that if they brew it, people will buy it."

The next Saturday, Miss Snot Face was back on the register and there was a full pot of decaf. She was ever so friendly when she sold me my coffee. Thirty minutes later, I was in the Kroger's parking lot. I was at least 100 yards and a key away from the nearest restroom when my bowels loosened.

Little Miss Snot Face had dosed the entire pot with Visine. I'm sure she believed that I was not aware of this old waitress trick for revenging on nasty customers. A few drops of Visine in a drink will cause one to lose control of their bowels. In most cases, said waitress gets to yuck it up while Mr. Grabby-Hands Non-Tipper hauls up his drawers and makes a run for the men's room. It can be dangerous though. With a certain heart condition it can lead to death. Too bad Miss Snot Face Blond didn't have a heart condition, I would have dosed her right back.

I thought about reporting her to Ken, but then she'd know she'd been successful. I decided to act as if nothing had happened to deny her any satisfaction. Since she had to dose the entire pot, she couldn't be sure she got it right.

She was particularly difficult to plan for. I knew little about her. I started walking my dog near the store when her shift was over to see what direction she went when she left. I did a bit of social engineering with one of the weekday clerks with whom I was chatty and learned her last name and looked her up in the directory. This was before Google Earth, Map Quest, Facebook and all those other internet sites that now make my task easier.

I drove by her house and noticed it was a charming cottage that was up a long, steep drive on West Fork Road. Opposite her drive was a gully with only a flimsy guardrail for protection.

I waited for the temperature to drop. I needed specific conditions, on a Saturday. Finally the weather shifted.

There is no place to park on West Fork Road. It twists and winds up through Mount Airy Forest with no berm. Shallow, rocky ditches line the uphill side with guardrails above a steep gully opposite. This meant I had to park a quarter mile away.

At 2:00 a.m., I turned off my engine and coasted down the hill. I pulled into her drive and unloaded eight boxes into the ditch, then coasted further down the hill to park in the drive of a repossessed home. I hiked back up the hill. I was wearing jeans and a navy blue hoodie with brown work gloves and hiking boots so I would blend into the darkness in case anyone drove by. Each box contained four gallons of water. One at a time I carried the boxes two thirds of the way up the drive, then trickled the water on the concrete, forming a long, wet path in freezing conditions. I worked slowly, emptying one box, repacking it with empty jugs, taking it down the drive, hauling up another box, building an ice patch layer by layer. When I was finished I jogged down to the car, drove it back up the hill, turned around, coasted down to Miss Snot Face's drive, loaded in the boxes of empty water jugs, then coasted the rest of the way down the hill. I drove to the Saint Boniface Church recycle bin and dumped the jugs and boxes. Naturally, I had ensured there were no fingerprints on the jugs.

Miss Snot Face did not arrive at work that day. The store opened two hours late and Ken was behind the counter. At that time, all he knew was that she hadn't responded when he called in at 7:00 a.m., and didn't answer her home phone or her cell. He had not been too

132

angry to remember to put a pot of decaf on. And I savored the taste and aroma as I wondered if she had been found yet.

The newspaper later reported that the broken guardrail had been called in mid-morning by a passing motorist. When police found her, she was comatose, her Karman Ghia rammed into a tree. By that time, the ice on her drive had melted so there was no evidence remaining.

Her broken bones took many months to heal. Her coma persisted for three years until her family finally decided to pull the plug. It gave me three years of pleasure to imagine her conscious, trapped inside her comatose body, and unable to move or communicate. Of course, I don't know if she was aware or not. But I understand sometimes people are aware in comas, so I liked to imagine her relatives sitting in her room, discussing pulling the plug while she was totally aware and incapable of begging them not to kill her.

I normally do not gloat over removals. This woman had been deliberately malicious towards me and deserved my ire. I had mixed feelings about Terry. His generosity and good nature were at odds with his smugly erroneous opinions. I'd considered removing him just so I wouldn't have to listen to right wing rhetoric over my coffee, but had always refrained because at heart he was a decent, if misguided individual.

Terry's removal was damage control. He was too smart, his memory was too good. His coma was not pleasurable. It was worrisome.

Chapter 14

Wednesday, May 25

"Catherine, are those daggers I see shooting out of your eyes?"

Catherine turned and smiled at Marie. The smile didn't reach her eyes and her expression was tense. "My goodness, what are you talking about?" Her voice was high and brittle.

"You seem unhappy with Detective Hottie." Marie's magenta bangs flopped over one eye.

"I don't see why he has to drag Viola up here. Lia's coming at the crack of dawn to avoid him. Lia doesn't need to be seeing that dog every day. I'm sure all it does is upset her."

"Has she told you that?"

Catherine sniffed. "She doesn't need to."

"I thought she was getting up at the crack of dawn to make your pavers."

"You make me sound like a slave driver."

Marie resorted to irony, "You? A slave driver? How could anyone think that? I'm sure she's still upset about Luthor, but she's also absorbed with your garden project. I think she's eager to get to the studio as early as she can."

"You think so?" Catherine relaxed.

"And I don't think she minds seeing Viola. She's always liked Viola. I think she sees her as the best part of Luthor."

"Perhaps you're right."

"So how is the garden coming?"

"I've got to keep my eyes on them every second, but it's going to be wonderful. You're coming to my party, aren't you? I'll be horribly upset if you don't."

"I wouldn't miss it. June 18th, isn't it?"

"Yes, and it's going to be so wonderful. We're going to have a sushi bar."

"You know I don't eat that stuff."

"A nice Asian girl like you? Afraid of a little smoked eel?"

"I'll stick with egg rolls, thank you."

"You really should broaden your palate."

Marie looked over Catherine's shoulder and spied Detective Dourson approaching. The man really must have a death wish. "What do you think, Detective? Should people eat raw fish?"

"Gollum seems fond of it."

"Gollum?" Catherine puzzled, "Who's Gollum?"

Marie laughed. "He means that creature in *Lord of the Rings*. Lived in a cave, crawled around with a fish flapping in his mouth. Didn't you ever see the movie?"

"How revolting."

"He lived a nice, long life," Peter added. "Maybe it was the fish and not the ring. As long as it's not Fugu, I'm in."

"As if," Catherine sniffed, "you can get fresh puffer fish in Cincinnati. Since you're such a big fan of sushi, Detective, you *must* come to my party."

"A party, Mrs. Laroux?"

"I'm celebrating my new garden with a Summer Solstice party on June 18th. We'll be starting at 5:00 p.m."

Marie turned to Peter in amazement. "You actually eat raw fish? You're from Kentucky. Why would a Kentucky boy eat raw fish?"

"I'm a Kentucky boy of unplumbed depths. I even know how to use chop sticks." He turned to Catherine. "I'd be delighted to attend your party. I see Viola is doing her daily duty, please excuse me, ladies." Peter trotted off while pulling a plastic bag out of his pocket.

"Weren't you just telling me you didn't want him at the park? Why did you invite him to your party?"

"Superior breeding never allows a little thing like personal feelings to interfere with one's social endeavors. I think a homicide detective will add intriguing cachet to my petite soiree, don't you agree?"

Marie shook her head. "You amaze me."

"Why, thank you, Darling."

Peter deposited Viola's latest 'present' in the trash, then spotted Nadine flinging balls for her Basset Hound, Rufus. She smiled in welcome as he walked up. "Hello, Detective. How are you and Viola getting along?"

Peter smiled back. "We're getting used to each other."

"I hope that means you're keeping her. She's a sweet dog."

"I'm leaning that way. How long have you had your Basset Hound?"

"Oh, he's not really a Basset Hound."

"No? What is he?"

"Well, he was Beagle, then the grandkids got hold of his ears, and well, this is what happened." Her expression was all sincerity and innocence.

"Why, Mrs. Moyers, I do believe butter would not melt in your mouth."

Nadine laughed. "Seriously, he's half Beagle. Lia calls him a Bagel. She says that sounds better than calling him a Beasett. I've had him for four years now. He's still got a lot of energy, so I've got to exercise him. But what about you, Detective?"

"What about me?"

"We're all wondering about you. How did a fascinating young man like yourself wind up so far from home, and still single?"

"Now I can't imagine you want to hear my sordid history."

"Small town scandal? What could be better? There's got to be a sad story about some girl who didn't deserve you."

"Can't imagine she'd see it that way."

"What was her name?" Nadine asked, priming the pump.

"It was Susan. I knew her in high school." Peter sighed, giving in to the inevitable.

"And you were going to get married." Nadine stated this as a fact.

"Yup. But she didn't like the idea of struggling while I was in college, so we waited. I got the bug to become a cop. She wanted a lawyer for a husband. She tried to wait me out. I told her she was welcome to be the lawyer in the family, but I think her ideas were more traditional. Finally she admitted that she couldn't handle being stuck with a cop's pay-grade. She married this guy we knew at high school. He used to be a football hero. Now he owns a furniture store and they do commercials together on late night TV. I like small towns, but it was feeling too small. So I came here."

"Has there been no one since?" Nadine's genuine sympathy was like a balm to the still sore spot on his heart.

"Well, once you're a cop, some folks think it's all you are. Some women chase the badge, and some are put off by it, but I haven't found anyone yet who really sees past it. Some guys live the badge. I believe in it, but it's not who I am."

"You poor man. No wonder you're attracted to Lia."

"Say again?"

"We can all see you're interested in her. An artist might be good for you. To an artist, every grain of sand on the beach is unique. And she has a life of her own. She doesn't need to turn anyone into her own personal Ken doll. We all love her, of course. You would be much better for her than that Luthor Morrissey was."

Peter shook his head. He guessed the dog park was it's own kind of small town.

"It's okay," she said brightly, "we approve."

~ ~ ~

Peter decided enough was enough. What was the phrase, "Beard a lion in its den?" He wondered if it were possible to beard a lioness. Did they have beards?

Lia knelt on the floor to inspect a mold when she heard a rap. Peter looked in through her open studio door.

"Can I come see?"

Lia was annoyed at the little trill of pleasure she felt when she heard his voice. "Yeah, sure."

"How are you doing?"

Lia shrugged. "As well as can be expected, I guess. Good days and bad days."

Peter got a mental image of pulling teeth from a lioness. Perseverance was needed, he decided. "How goes the project?"

"It's coming along. We've got one more set of pavers to do, then while those are curing, we'll do the bench."

"I didn't know you were going to make a bench, too."

"Madam must have a proper bench from which to peruse her very expensive koi and achieve Nirvana. Lucky for us, it adds another eighteen hundred dollars to the price tag."

"So what are you doing now?"

"Getting ready to un-mold these puppies."

"What keeps the molds from sticking?" Peter asked.

"They have fancy mold release sprays. I find a liberal coat of vegetable oil does just fine." She carefully lifted the square of styrofoam from around the finished paver, set it aside, then turned the stepping stone over and peeled off the contact paper. Brilliantly colored bits of tile stared back at Peter.

"That's amazing."

"Thank you."

"Hard to believe that's busted up tile and concrete. What happens next?"

"Today I inspect the surface, clean off any stray bits of concrete, run a file around the top edge. Then they get stacked in that corner where they get soaked down and covered with plastic to hold the water in." She gestured to the amorphous, plastic-draped pile behind her.

"Why do you keep them wet?"

"The longer you keep it wet, the stronger concrete becomes. It's a chemical reaction"

"I didn't know that."

Lia carried the paver over to her work table and set it down. Peter noticed she had set up a six foot folding table alongside it.

"Can I help?"

"Sure, I'll pop the molds, you set the pavers on the tables."

They worked silently with a pleasant, satisfying rhythm. Peter noted that it was an easy silence. He chose not to break it until both tables were full of concrete circles. "I haven't seen you at the park lately."

Lia gestured at the loaded tables. "I've been on Dawn Patrol at the park. I have to get in here and get cracking early. Mistress Catherine is a demanding taskmaster."

He looked directly into her jade eyes. "Is that the only reason?"

She looked away, bit her lip. "I've been wanting to let things settle a bit. Your last bombshell was a lot to take in."

"I'm sorry for that."

"You're just the messenger. It's not like *you* shot him."

"I can still be sorry."

"Thanks. I've been racking my brains and I still can't make sense of it. I still can't believe I never realized what Luthor was up to. I thought he was spending all that time writing. No wonder the book never went anywhere."

Peter considered what else Luthor had been up to that Lia still didn't know about. He couldn't tell her since Catherine had a right to privacy. But if he could, he wouldn't. He didn't think Lia was self-destructive enough to take a hammer to all Catherine's pavers, but it would not improve working relations. He imagined her embedding spikes into the bench.

She looked at him with a wry twist to her mouth. "I feel so guilty. I feel relieved that Luthor is out of my life but it was awful the way it happened and I feel guilty that I'm not grieving more." She took a deep breath. "And then I'm angry that he was pulling all this behind my back and I want to kill him. And then I realize that I can't because he's already dead. And then I feel guilty again."

"Sounds confusing."

"It is. I don't know if it's good that I have this huge, repetitive project that I can do while I'm not thinking clearly, or if it's a bad thing because it gives me too much time to obsess about it."

"It'll sort itself out."

"I hope so. So how is the investigation going?"

"I think I'm supposed to say, 'We are pursuing all leads.'"

"Are there leads?"

"Not really. We have questions, but nothing that places anyone in the park at 2:00 in the morning. Forensics hasn't turned up anything on Luthor, his car or the gun. Anything they picked up in the lot is useless because I'm convinced Luthor's murderer was a park regular, so their trace could be anywhere and we couldn't say when they left it."

"I just can't get over that. I keep looking at people, wondering who it could be, and I can't imagine anyone I know killing someone."

"Just about anyone will kill someone under the right conditions. Sometimes it's a matter of figuring out their conditions."

"Well, self-defense, sure, if someone's got their hands around your neck. But to plan something out like this? And be able to pull the trigger? That's cold. It's inhuman and evil."

"What about self-defense of a different sort? What if Luthor threatened someone's security or position in some way?"

"How could he possibly do that?"

"I know this is hard, but what if we haven't uncovered all of his girlfriends? What if one was married?" Peter couldn't reveal his interview with Catherine, but he could put a bug in her ear.

"Luthor in an affair with a married woman at the park? The only person I can think of would be Catherine, and she has children older than Luthor."

"Did you and Luthor always go at the same time? Is it possible he knew people there that you don't know?"

"It's unlikely. Some of my friends go at different times and they would have mentioned if they'd seen Luthor. But you've been up there. It's dirty and muddy and people wear their grungiest clothes, and they're walking around, picking up poop. It's not exactly conducive to steamy affairs."

"I thought there had been some marriages between people who met up there."

Lia searched her mind for how to explain. "You see the same people all the time, and the crowd isn't big enough to easily avoid someone. When two people are on the outs, everyone knows it. When people hang together, everyone knows it. If Luthor was friendly with someone he met up there and then, say he dumped her or he was going to create a problem for her, everybody would notice. Like they've all noticed Catherine doesn't like you for some reason. She likes all men, so how is it she doesn't like you? Did she make a pass at you? You turn her down?"

Lia had just made a flying leap and landed too close for comfort. "You'd have to ask her. Anna suggested I'm not paying her proper attention and beyond that, my investigation is spreading bad energy all over her pavers. Rumor is, I'm the reason you're in and out at dawn these days, though Jim says it's because you're so busy with your pavers."

"Goodness, you've certainly found your way into the grapevine." She sighed. "Mostly, it's the project. Part of it's you because every time we talk it seems things get weirder. Part of it's them. I'm having a hard time dealing with the idea that one of them killed someone and could even be a serial killer. With that, and everything you've told me about Luthor, I'm wondering about my own judgment. I don't know what to think. It's easier just to come here and arrange tile scraps."

"I guess I can't blame you. I'm really sorry about all this. I wish we could find your cell phone, that would clarify things. It hasn't turned up?"

"No, I would have called you. I need to get a new one, I haven't gotten around to it yet."

"Lia, I know this isn't easy." She snorted at the understatement. Despite the scoffing sound effect, Peter saw her eyes glisten. She looked up at him helplessly as silent tears began to trail down both cheeks. Peter felt that part of him, the professional distance he facetiously called his "inner Jack Webb," crumble into dust. He tentatively reached out and gently stroked her cheek. Lia turned on her stool and leaned into his chest, sobbing in earnest. He stood there while she wrapped her arms around him.

He stroked her hair while she buried her face in his shirt, soaking it with tears. They stayed like that for several minutes. Then her grip on him lightened, and he felt her tug his shirt out of his jeans, slide her hands beneath it. Her cheek rubbed back and forth across his shirt. He reached behind his back to twine his hands with hers and pull them between him and her. He hooked another stool with his foot and dragged it over, sitting so that he could look in her eyes. They were bright, fluid, and woeful.

"This is quickly becoming improper."

"Don't care." Lia's tone was heartbreaking and petulant.

"I do. I'm afraid you'll abuse me and cast me aside." He realized his thumbs were chafing her palms.

She sighed. "Did you ever feel so intensely that it was hard to live in your skin? Like you were about to come out of it?"

"Is that how you feel right now?"

"I can't stand it. I can't stand thinking about any of this anymore. Will you please shut the door?"

"Are you sure?"

"Throw the latch."

Peter paused to consider. The timing was awful. He was on duty. They were in her studio, someone could interrupt. These thoughts flitted ineffectually against his brain like moths outside a lit window. He watched, as if outside himself, as he latched the door and walked back to where Lia still sat on her stool. She picked up his shirt and lay her cheek against his taut abdomen, then kissed it, tracking across his firm flesh. He pulled the tie off her ponytail and buried his hands in her hair. They stayed like that for a long moment, absorbing the feel of flesh on flesh. He drew her up and kissed her, softly, on her brow, her cheeks, the corners of her mouth, the spot on her neck just below her ear. His hands stroked her back, kneading her flesh, crushing her against him. She opened her lips and he captured them, teasing the inside of her mouth with his tongue while she reeled and her knees weakened. She pulled away and gestured to a pile of blankets in the corner. She wordlessly pulled off her shirt, exposing pert, rosy-tipped breasts.

~ ~ ~

Lia lay with her head against Peter's chest. It was a long, lean chest with a flurry of dark hair arrowing down past his navel. She traced one finger up and down it, combed her fingers through the curls. Her right leg was thrown across his thighs. "Thank you."

He kissed the top of her head. "For what?"

"For going with the moment."

"It was some moment."

"It was a very nice moment," Lia agreed.

"Are you hungry? I'm starving."

"After that, I could eat a horse."

"Don't let my friends in the Mounted Police hear you say that."

"Chinese or pizza?"

"Those are my only choices?"

"Those are the only choices that deliver. I don't want to go out into the world just yet."

"Me neither. Are you going to let me romance you?"

"Please?"

"Okay, since you asked so nice."

144

She gave him a mild thump on his biceps with her fist. "You know what I meant."

"The Kentucky in me couldn't resist. Cincinnati is the only city in the world that has to say 'please' instead of 'pardon me.' Who made that up, anyway?"

"Not sure. Probably Cincinnatus."

"Couldn't have been him, he never lived here."

"So now you're going to split hairs."

"Seriously, can I call you on the phone and maybe take you to dinner or is this just a 'thanks for being here, but let's pretend it didn't happen' kind of thing?"

"Why do you want to know?"

"If this is a one-time event, if you're just going to use me and throw me away, I want Chinese and you're buying."

"We're getting pizza. We'll go dutch."

"You really set on pizza?"

"No, but I don't want you to think you were just handy."

"How about we get Kung Pao Shrimp and I'll call you anyway?"

"I have a question to ask you." Lia turned earnest.

"Fire away."

"Guys get interested in me because I'm creative and after we start dating they get upset because I spend time doing art."

"That sounds idiotic."

"I always thought so. It's part of me. I've had art since I was five and some guy comes along and starts pouting because I have work to do."

"You going to bring your easel to dinner?"

"Don't see why I would."

"I like your paintings. Your exes were really stupid. Does this mean you know me well enough to sing Viola's Pee Song for me?"

"Gosh, I don't know, you have yet to buy me dinner."

145

"I hear it resembles Doris Day singing 'Do the Hokey Pokey' with a touch of Texas soul yodel."

"What? Who said?"

"I've been sworn to secrecy. Apparently you were overheard when you thought no one was around."

"I refuse to comment."

"Don't pout. They were very complimentary."

"Right."

"I've been singing to Viola, but I'm afraid I'm not so original."

"Oh, really?"

"If she needs to do a number one, I sing 'Louie, Louie,' you know, 'We gotta go now.'"

"Fascinating. So what do you do for a number two?"

"She gets the *Star Wars* theme. Dump-dump; Dump dump dump dump dump; Dump dump dump dump dump; Dump dump dump dump;

Lia shook her head, laughing into his chest. "Viola's got to be mortified."

"Don't know about her, but the guys at the station are getting their yucks. Especially when I do the 'Aye-yi-yi-yi' during 'Louie, Louie.'"

"Detective Dourson, a poet, you're not."

"What can I say?" He shrugged comically.

"You can say, 'Hey, Lia, what's the number for the Chinese place on Ludlow?'"

"Why would I say that?"

"Because I don't have a phone."

Chapter 15

Thursday, May 26

"Goodness, it's the Phantom Artist."

"Hello, Anna," Lia said as she climbed up on the table.

"Running late today?"

"Slept in."

Anna eyed Lia carefully. "You certainly look relaxed."

"Do I?"

"Yes, you do. What's happened?"

"Nothing's happened."

"Uh-huh. Does nothing drive a Chevy Blazer and stand about six foot two?"

"Where would you get an idea like that?"

"I knew it! Deets! Give!"

"No way."

"You're no fun."

"Go find your own guy."

"Don't let Catherine find out. She'll figure you broke him in just for her."

"Catherine? She's old enough to be his mother!"

"Won't stop her from trying." Kita ran up and leaned against Anna, shoving her head under Anna's hand for a scratch just as Bailey joined them. "Bailey, dear, our Lia's been a busy girl."

"Really? What have I missed?"

"Check the rosy cheeks, the sparkle in her eye . . . ."

"I'm not talking to you two."

"It's okay," Bailey said, "I'm utterly clueless. You can talk to me."

"Anna thinks I have a love life."

"I gathered that. Is she right?"

"Don't know. Maybe. Trying not to think about it. Anna thinks Catherine will try to steal him from me."

"Maybe, maybe not. She's not taken with Detective Hottie lately. That is who we're not talking about, isn't it? If Catherine decided he's distracting you, she's going to be even more put out with him. Of course, she may decide she has to seduce him to stop him from interfering with your work."

"Bailey," Lia laughed, "you're so bad."

"Does he have a brother? I'd like to be distracted, too. I'd even settle for a cousin."

~ ~ ~

Brent eyed Peter curiously from the next desk. "Why so glum, Dourson?"

"I'm in a weird situation, Brent. Things have heated up with Lia."

"If you're upset about that, you really *do* have a problem."

"Not that. She doesn't know about Catherine and Luthor. Technically, she doesn't have a right to know, and I'm not at liberty to tell her. And if she did know, I don't know how she'd feel about finishing Catherine's garden, and I know this project is important to her. But at some point it'll come out and she's going to hate me for not telling her."

"Ouch. Would it be insensitive of me to suggest that you get as much as you can before that happy day?"

"I thought you were an evolved, new millennium kind of guy."

"That's what you get for believing stereotypes. Are you into profiling too? Rousted any innocent Muslims lately?"

"I leave that for the street cops. So how do I handle this?"

"What happened to your oh-so-noble and admirable decision to keep your distance until Morrisey's case was resolved?"

Peter sighed. "She was crying, and I guess I was patting her or something and it just happened."

"Ah, it just happened. A very popular defense."

"Shove it."

"Didn't think you swung that way. You going to tell Lia about your bi-sexuality?"

Peter rolled his eyes. "Any ideas?"

Brent considered his dilemma. "Not much you can do. Wear kevlar?"

"Funny."

"She likely to turn clingy?"

Peter shook his head. "Doubtful."

"How easy would it be to retreat some?"

"She'll do that for me. All I have to do is stand still."

"Don't get all wounded about it; her boyfriend just died. You don't have much choice but to let her work it out. Is she reasonable?"

"Well, sure."

"Then she'll eventually realize that you can't gossip about cases."

"It's that 'eventually' that worries me. Like how long is 'eventually' going to be? This could get awfully messy."

"You're a detective. Haven't you detected that life is awfully messy?"

"Since when did you become a shrink?"

~ ~ ~

The card read, "Rare and beautiful, like you." She traced the edges of the orchid's pale violet petals with her index finger. It was potted, not cut. Had he figured out that she hated cut flowers? Or was it just a sale on potted plants at Home Depot? Either way, it was thoughtful and beautiful. It would make a great painting.

Lia brought the plant into her studio. The pot was a vintage glazed ceramic in a lovely pale blue-green, no Home Depot job, not from the florists, either. The retro pot might have belonged to someone's grandmother. Extra marks for repotting it, and double word points for the choice of pot.

She set the pot on her work table, turned it ever so slightly so the light made a strong statement. She pulled out her digital camera and snapped off a couple dozen pictures, playing with the scale and framing, adjusting the pot to change the way the light hit it. When she was satisfied, she pulled out a square canvas and set up her easel, squeezing a smear of burnt umber onto her palette, mixing it with a dribble of linseed oil to make a pale brown. She pulled out her oldest brush, a size four with the bristles worn down almost to the ferule, and dipped it in the tinted oil.

She drew quickly, exploding shapes onto the square canvas, pulling the eye into the center of the flower. She used a rag dipped in oil to erase lines she didn't like, then redrew them. When she was happy, she covered the background in a glaze of bottle green, using a rag to pull out pigment so the canvas would show through. She laid out her paints and mixed delicate hues, cream, pink, violet, lavender, pale fuchsia, and used these to model the elegant petals. She stood back and absorbed her work, feeling a deep satisfaction. The core of the flower was luminous but partly hidden. A mystery that enticed.

"That's wonderful. You just did that?"

She smiled and turned. Peter leaned against the doorjamb, looking positively edible. "I was inspired."

"So you liked your gift?"

"It's lovely. Where did you get the pot? I could hit estate sales for months and not find one like it."

"My eighty year-old neighbor, Alma, has a green thumb and never throws anything away. She's lived in the same house for fifty years. She knew exactly what was needed."

"Did she provide the orchid, too?"

"I can't tell a lie. She did do. She felt sorry for me."

"You'll have to introduce her to me, so I can thank her."

"Don't I get any thanks?"

"Not sure you deserve any, taking advantage of a nice old lady like that."

"I'm hurt. Deeply."

"Play your cards right and maybe someone will want to kiss it and make it better."

"Really?"

"Then again, maybe not." She eyed him consideringly. "You don't look like much of a card player, Kentucky Boy." She gave him a hug and leaned her head against his chest. He wrapped his arms around her waist and they swayed gently.

Birds trilled.

"Nuts." Lia reached into her hip pocket and fished out a cell phone, looked at the screen, pushed "accept." "Where are you? . . . Shit. I'm sorry, I got distracted. I'll be there in ten minutes. Can you wait that long? . . . See you." She hit "end" and put it back in her pocket.

"Find your phone?"

"New one. Bailey made me get it. She also programmed the ring tone. Turns out the Woo Woo Queen is a techno-geek. I'm sorry, I was supposed to meet Bailey at the greenhouse five minutes ago to pick out plants for Catherine's garden."

"I was going to ask if you wanted lunch, but it looks like you're busy."

"Pretty much. Rain check?"

"Counting on it." She cleaned her brushes quickly and hustled Peter out of the studio.

"You know," Peter offered, "I could drive you to the greenhouse and take both of you to lunch after."

"Seriously?"

"Sure. Why not. Does Bailey like Indian? We could go to Dusmesh."

"Great idea."

They were more than ten minutes. Bailey's eyebrows rose when she saw Lia's company. "Is this your distraction?"

"No," Lia laughed, "my distraction was the present someone left at my studio door. Peter just happened along right before you called. I was painting and totally forgot we were meeting. So where are we at?"

"Catherine's making me insane." Bailey looked at Peter. "You're like a priest, right? You can't repeat anything we say when the client isn't around."

"My lips are sealed." Peter crossed his heart solemnly.

"What's the problem, Bailey?" Lia asked.

"She wants an aromatherapy garden, and she wants all native plants and she wants a lot of big, showy blossoms. In other words, she thinks we can somehow magically make everything she wants into a therapeutic plant with Ohio ancestry."

"Ah. The Princess from Jupiter waved her scepter and declared it so, did she? What are your inclinations?"

"I say we let it all go to Chickory and Chickweed and remind her they're native herbs," Bailey pouted.

"You might get away with that if you put in a Cone-Flower or two, Maybe some Four-O'Clocks?"

"I like native plants. I just don't think they'll be showy enough for Dame Catherine."

"So we have to ignore the bullshit and figure out not only what will make her happy but also how to present it so that she knows she's happy."

"Exactly. Damn it, I really wanted to do the high vibration garden."

"So let's walk and talk. By the way, Peter's taking us to Dusmesh for lunch after this."

Bailey turned to Peter. "In that case, you can stay."

Peter trailed along as Lia and Bailey discussed color, growing season, conditions. They debated Trillium, Dutchman's Breeches, Turtle Head, Fairy Wand, Butterfly Weed, Maiden-Hair Fern, Jack-in-the-Pulpit, and many others with names he'd never heard before, seeking the right combination to encourage butterflies and hummingbirds as well as provide blooms all spring and summer.

"The thing is," Bailey said, "she's going to have to choose between aromatherapy and native plants. She can't have both."

"Steering her towards native plants is the responsible thing to do. Think she'll be okay giving up the aromatherapy angle if she's got hummingbirds to play with?"

"Possibly. Too bad we've missed spring blooms. She's not going to fully appreciate this until next year. The plants won't be established for her party. Planting a native garden is more complex than cramming in flats of whatever annuals are in bloom so you have a nice show."

"I have a thought," Peter interrupted.

Bailey and Lia turned in unison and looked at Peter with owl eyes. They'd forgotten he was there. "Yeah?"

"If I'm hearing this right, the big issue is that there won't be a big showy garden full of flowers for this party."

Bailey responded. "Pretty much. It's more complicated than that, but if it weren't for the party, her expectations would be a lot more reasonable, and she'd be more open to reality."

"What if you bring in some color?"

"How would we do that?"

"Don't people raise butterflies for special events? What if you set up a tent of mosquito netting, like a dining canopy, and released butterflies in there. It would be like the conservatory's annual butterfly show in her back yard."

Lia and Bailey frowned at each other. "The island, maybe?" Lia ventured. "People could sit on the bench."

"None of her friends have ever done it. It could work."

Lia grinned at Peter. "I knew there was a reason I let you come along."

"And I thought it was free food for the starving artists."

"Hey," Bailey admonished, "we'll take the food, too."

"She's going to love this idea," Lia relished.

"Shall we give you credit, Peter?" Bailey asked.

"Umm . . . No, don't do that. She doesn't seem to like me lately."

"Why is that?"

"Good question, Bailey. Leave me out of it. You can take the credit."

"Why does Bailey get the credit?" Lia demanded.

"You got an orchid. I thought Bailey could get the credit. Unless you want to give your orchid to Bailey?"

Lia raised one eyebrow and gave Peter an evil look.

"Watching you brilliant, creative geniuses work has given me an appetite. Are you ladies ready for Palak Paneer?"

~ ~ ~

Peter got such a kick, watching Lia and Bailey bounce ideas as they sat at a white linen covered table and sampled from the buffet. He almost forgot he was working. He didn't like being sneaky, but the opportunity to observe one of Lia's closest friends was potentially too illuminating to pass up.

Could Bailey be his killer? She was smart and organized enough. She had no love for Luthor. But what would her motive be? While Luthor's girlfriends seemed to keep popping out of the woodwork, he couldn't see Bailey involved with him. She wasn't his type. Could it have been blackmail? Just because Catherine gave Luthor money doesn't mean that was the cash in the Lazy Boy. Or, going with the psycho theory, perhaps he wore the same kind of shoes as the kid who bullied her in second grade. Perhaps he should put motive aside.

Catherine had motive, but he just couldn't see it. She was used to having other people deal with the nastier aspects of life for her. Lia and Bailey's description of her suggested someone self-involved and flighty, too lacking in the awareness of others and of practical realities to have crafted so precise a scenario as Luthor's death. No, Catherine would have hired her pool boy to do it, then been astonished when he cut a deal and ratted her out. Unless, following Brent's scenario, she just got pissed, hunted Luthor down and drilled him into swiss cheese.

But Bailey. Lia swore the 'Woo Woo Queen' would never commit murder due to the karma she would incur. Could it be an act? The person he was looking for would have an act of some kind.

155

"So what do you want to bet Catherine tries to hire Luella Zuckerman to talk to the butterflies during her party?" Lia's comment brought Peter back to the present and his Saag Vindaloo.

"Can you talk to butterflies?" Peter inquired.

Bailey snorted. "If anyone can, it would be Luella. But she'd tell you that butterflies wouldn't have much to say except 'Sweet! Pretty! Flower!'" Her high-pitched imitation had them all laughing.

"Huh," Peter said. "So what's your next step?"

"We take Catherine down to Enright Avenue to see the native gardens there and get her expectations in line with reality. We sell her on the butterflies by showing her pretty pictures," Lia explained in between bites of her frozen Mango Chat.

"Sounds like you think Catherine's pretty clueless."

"It's not that she's dumb," mused Bailey, "She just doesn't bother to think. She's a new moon baby with Venus in Gemini, always off on the newest fad and barely scraping the surface."

"Like those butterflies?" Peter asked.

"That's it! We'll tell her the butterflies remind us of her. She'll love it." Lia responded. She grinned at Peter and his heart stopped, just for a second. "You, Sir, are brilliant."

"Why all the strategizing and manipulation?"

"Alas, Detective," Bailey mourned, "not being public servants, we are subject to the whims of our patrons. We have to catch her at the right phase of her infatuation and somehow keep her focused until the project is complete. Otherwise, she'll want to scrap it for some new idea, and not want to pay for what we've done. With Catherine it means preempting any stray thought that's doomed to lead her off the path, so to speak. We have to constantly appeal to her ego. It's exhausting."

"You've really thought this out."

"Survival, Detective, pure survival."

Bailey was obviously a planner, aware of subtleties. And if it was Bailey, it would kill Lia.

Chapter 16

Monday, May 30

"Damn." Peter set the receiver down gently, despite the urge to slam it.

"What's up?" Brent inquired from the next desk.

"I thought we were okay, but she's not taking my calls again."

"Okay, Potter."

"Huh?"

"You're in the middle of a Harry Potter scenario."

"What does some kid with a weird scar have to do with me?"

"Literature holds the meaning of life, Dourson. This is just like book five, *Order of the Phoenix*. Harry's got this big crush on Cho Chang, and she likes him back. But she keeps acting all wiggy because her last boyfriend was killed by Voldemort in book four, and Harry was there."

"You think Morrisey was killed by Voldemort?"

"Of course not, that would be too easy. But I think Lia's acting like Cho Chang. Harry blew it with Cho because he didn't understand her moods and, hey, he had Hermione and Ron to hang with."

"So you're saying I'm an unfeeling jerk?"

"No, I'm just saying she's got to work it out and if that seems like too much trouble to you, then maybe you really belong with Ginny Weasley instead."

"Who's Ginny Weasley?"

"Do you really want a run-down of all the chicks in Harry Potter? Maybe I could hook you up with that tramp, Lavender Brown."

"Go away, Brent. Get a real girlfriend."

"Careful, or I'll sick Hermione on you. She's got one wicked right hook."

~ ~ ~

"Don't you look all down in the dumps. What's the matter?" Jim joined Lia on top of her favorite picnic table, where she was throwing tennis balls for Honey. Fleece sat in front of her, in expectation of petting.

"I feel guilty." She leaned over and gave Fleece a scratch behind the ears.

"You couldn't possibly be guilty of anything worth feeling bad about."

"I feel so weird. Luthor just died and I'm already having feelings for someone else. That's just wrong."

"Did you really love Luthor?"

"I'm not sure. That's what I feel guilty about. But then I get all mad because now I'm finding out he had other girlfriends and was getting lots of money from somewhere I didn't know about."

"If you didn't love him, looks like there was good reason."

"He acted like he just couldn't live without me."

"Sounds manipulative to me. If he hadn't died, would you be feeling guilty about seeing someone new?"

"I guess not."

"I'm sorry he shot himself."

"But that's just it, Jim, he didn't shoot himself."

"What are you talking about?"

"Damn. I shouldn't have said anything. It just slipped out. It's not public knowledge, but Peter says they think he was murdered."

"Why do they think that?"

"Because he was left-handed and Luthor was shot on the right side. And he avoided guns. And I think he would have been too chicken to pull the trigger anyway."

"Oh."

"Don't tell anyone, please? Peter thinks someone here at the park did it. He says you have to know this place to think of it as a rendezvous point, and they had to know me to steal my cell phone. Someone sent Luthor a text from my phone right before he came here that night."

"We're all suspects?" Jim asked, troubled.

"I'm not, at least Peter says I'm not. I guess I should be. He's only got my word that I lost my phone. I don't know what they think about anyone else."

"That's a lot of people. What reason would anyone have had for killing Luthor?"

"Peter thinks it was a psycho. But we don't have any psychos. Kooks and eccentrics, but no psychos unless you want to count the weird guy who used to bring his Akita last spring."

"How long have you been carrying this around?" he inquired, now concerned.

"Peter told me almost three weeks ago. I'm afraid, Jim. If it's a crazy person with no motive except they're crazy, doesn't that mean they can do it again?"

"Are they certain it's murder?"

"Certain enough to have Peter investigating. I keep thinking they're mistaken, but then I remember about that text message they say came from the phone I can't find. If he shot himself, then where's my phone, and who sent that text? There's no other explanation. I don't want to look at my friends and wonder if they shot my boyfriend. Right now, you're one of the only people I trust. I hate feeling this way."

"Who have you told?"

"Just you, Jim. Didn't mean to, it sort of busted out. I despise secrets, and I'm sorry I dumped this on you. Look, you won't tell anyone, will you?"

"No, I won't, unless you say it's okay."

Just then CarGo and Rufus bounded up, tongues hanging out in canine good cheer that refuted Lia's mood. Lia ruffled CarGo's neck as she watched Anna and Nadine approach. Jealous, Fleece crowded in.

"So serious over here!" Nadine announced. "What are you two cooking up on the back side of the park?"

"Lia's wrestling with some devils today," Jim responded.

"I'm so sorry, can I hit one of them over the head for you? Bean him with CarGo's tennis ball?" Anna offered.

"This must be about that nice detective," Nadine said.

"How'd you guess?" Lia asked.

"You young girls. It's always about a man, and with him around, who else could it be?" Nadine patted her on the knee.

"If you're so smart, what am I feeling bad about?"

"Well, I'm sure you haven't done anything truly heinous. I think it has something to do with your back-to-the-Mayflower Puritan roots."

"What are you talking about, Nadine?" Anna inquired.

"Lia's feeling bad about feeling good."

"Uh . . . well . . . it's just not that simple," Lia mumbled.

161

"Sweetie, feel bad about Luthor if you need to. But don't let that stop you from feeling good about Peter," Anna advised.

"It's awfully confusing."

"Of course it is," Nadine sympathized. "But do you really want to tell the charming detective to go away until you figure it out? Do you suppose he'll still be twiddling his thumbs when you've tidied your life up?"

"Nadine," Jim interjected, "that's not fair to either of them."

"Nadine's right," Anna asserted. "Life isn't fair. But Lia, don't let bad timing get in the way of your happiness. Don't make an obstacle out of Luthor dying."

"You think Luthor dying is an obstacle?"

"He made you unhappy when you were together. Don't let him continue to make you unhappy now that he's gone."

"He's not gone, dammit, he's *dead*! Sorry, I didn't mean to yell at you. I just need some space." Lia pushed off the table and called Honey and Chewy to her as she stalked back towards the woods.

"Oh, dear. I seem to have missed the mark."

"You're usually more tactful, Anna."

"Yes, Jim, I usually am."

~ ~ ~

Lia was halfway down the gorge behind the dog park when Kita ran up the path and play-bowed to Honey. Honey barked and bowed back, then chased Kita back down the hill. Lia heard Bailey calling to Kita from the bottom of the trail. It looked like company was inevitable. She made her way carefully down the steep incline. When she reached the bottom, she found Bailey sitting on a log by the creek with a book.

"Hey, what are you reading?" Lia asked as she joined Bailey on the log.

"It's a book about reincarnation and soul-groups."

"Soul-groups? What are those?" Lia asked, glad to have something to talk about besides Peter Dourson and her personal life.

"Soul-groups contract to support each other by performing certain roles in various incarnations," Bailey launched into her explanation.

"How does that work?"

"Families are often soul-groups. In another lifetime, your mother might have been your sister or your child, or even your husband. Sometimes it's kinda crazy."

"How so?"

"The harder the life, the more you can learn. So sometimes souls decide to come into life handicapped in some way, physically, economically, emotionally."

"I can see that."

"So you decide you want to experience living in squalor in a war-torn third-world country. Some of your soul-group is likely to come along with you."

"You mean instead of opting for a life of leisure on the Riviera."

"Exactly. So souls are choosing to go into situations that are toxic and even dangerous to support each other."

"That would be a true friend," Lia commented.

"Now suppose someone wanted to increase their compassion by having a traumatic experience, say, being a rape victim."

"Someone would volunteer for that? Sounds harsh."

"And brave. Well, they would then contract with a member of their soul-group to be the rapist."

"You're kidding me," Lia said, appalled.

"Truth. According to this book anyway," Bailey shrugged.

"But wouldn't the rapist be messing with their own karma?"

"I haven't gotten to that part of the book yet, but I think they might get special dispensation, since it's a soul agreement that serves the higher good."

"So you're saying that someone who gets raped literally asked for it? That's whacked!"

"Not all the time, only sometimes, and that's over-simplifying."

"I don't know about that book, Bailey."

"I haven't made up my mind yet. It's certainly thought-provoking," Bailey responded.

"So you're saying we might have asked Catherine to come into our lives to make us crazy?"

"Very possibly."

"Geezlepete."

~ ~ ~

Something's up. I don't know what it is, but things are not settling down the way they should now that Terry's out of the picture. Is it just Lia's confusion about Detective Dourson, or is there more to the story? There's too much gossip at the park, people hanging out without anything else to do but take small inferences and blow them into raging tsunamis of rumor. Perhaps this was a dangerous pool for me to dip in. Nothing can be done about that now, but keep still and watch. Then again, maybe there's another way to look at this.

Chapter 17

This time the pot sitting outside her studio door held a cactus with a single coral bloom. She sat it on her table, pulled up a stool and sat down. She glowered at the spiny plant, jerked out her phone. Peter answered on the fourth ring.

"Are you suggesting I'm prickly?"

"Hello to you, too. How are you?"

"I'm wondering what it means when a guy gives you a cactus."

"You don't like it?"

"I don't know yet."

"I thought it was pretty cool when Alma told me how rare it is when they bloom."

"Hmmm."

"She also told me about that plant at Krohn Conservatory that blooms every hundred years and stinks like rotting meat, but I didn't think you'd go for that one."

"It wouldn't fit in my studio, anyway. They had to pull out part of the roof last time it bloomed."

"If you don't like the cactus, I'm sure Alma wouldn't mind taking it back. She has a big heart for rejected strays."

Lia gently brushed the tips of the spines with her finger. "Are you an Indian giver now?"

"I can't win, can I?"

"Probably not."

"Will you paint this one, too?"

"Maybe."

"If I buy you lunch, will you tell me what's wrong?"

Lia sighed. "I really like you, Peter."

"But?"

"I keep freaking out about Luthor being murdered. I hate what I'm finding out about him and what that says about me. And I can't take looking at all my friends and wondering who's going to pull out a knife. Everything is really squirrelly, you know? It makes it hard for me to think about dating."

"I wish I could make it go away. I'm almost sorry I told you about Luthor. But I couldn't stand to see you blame yourself."

"What about your investigation?"

Now it was Peter's turn to sigh. "It's going nowhere. I've been told to stop spending time on it, since there's no physical evidence at the scene to link to a suspect. We've got nothing unless your phone shows up. And if he was as smart as I think, he pulled the SIM card and tossed it."

"Will he do it again?"

"I don't know. I wish I could say it isn't likely, but since we don't know the motive, we can't speculate when, where or even if he'll strike again. It would be a very good idea to never agree to meet someone alone in an isolated area, especially if the invite came by text message."

~ ~ ~

The painting, when it was done, had an edgy feeling to it. Delicate tissue petals set against vicious spikes. A Jeckyll and Hyde kind of thing. Translucent reds and oranges against dull, dense greens. A study in contrasts. Lia thought it summed up how she felt, the tension of jagged edges of pain and mistrust against fluttery warmth.

Time made things no clearer to her. She felt awkward about Peter, about having jumped him on impulse and now having to deal with him. He wasn't hard to deal with, exactly. She just didn't know him and wasn't sure what his expectations were, or what she wanted. It had been a mistake, that afternoon in the studio. He was cute, but not exactly her type. He seemed to be a picket fence kind of guy. What did they have in common? After everything she found out about Luthor, maybe she shouldn't be with her type anyway. But what did it say about her that she hadn't been aware of the things Luthor had been up to? That she had been attracted to Luthor in the first place? Maybe she had no business being with anybody.

~ ~ ~

Lia finished the meditation bench and helped Bailey plant the garden while Jose excavated the pond and compacted sand on the twisting path. Next they would set in edging, lay the stones, then spread crushed limestone over the empty spaces in the path. She welcomed the long days and hard, sweaty work. It kept her from thinking about Peter too much.

She wasn't thinking about Peter . . . much. She *was* thinking about his warning. She turned to Jose and had a long talk about personal protection. Somehow she couldn't see herself carrying a taser all the time. Or a gun, or a snap-out baton. Surely she didn't need to be afraid, did she?

Then there was the problem with Bailey. Catherine was Catherine. And Catherine's frequent oversight was setting Bailey's nerves on edge. Not that Catherine wouldn't set anyone's nerves on edge, but in the past, Bailey had been able to toss off a joke, roll those protuberant eyes of hers, and stay focussed. Now she was moody. Lia worried that she was going to blow up on the job. Some days she was pumped up and raring to go, others she seemed like she could hardly crawl out of bed. And some days, her mood turned on a dime, usually after a visit from Catherine. Bailey said it was just Catherine, and as soon as they finished the garden, she'd be better. Lia decided to take it on faith and let it go. Catherine was more inclined to talk to her anyway. So she buffered the two as best she could, and crossed her fingers that they'd make it to the end.

She saw Peter at the park. They had lunch, caught a Christian Bale movie, and by tacit agreement did not mention the afternoon they'd spent rolling on the floor in Lia's studio. Peter figured they were just catching up, doing things they should have done before rolling on the floor, and when the time was right they'd get back around to it. Peter had hunted as a young man in the Kentucky hills. He knew the value of waiting.

Peter had been pulled off the Morrisey case to chase down car-jackers operating on Hamilton Avenue. "Cheeky bastards," he said. "District Five is less than half a mile away."

"Do Kentucky boys say 'cheeky'?"

"They do if they've spent any time around Terry. How is he?"

"No change. Donna goes to see him every day and she reads Bernard Cornwell to him." Peter gave her a quizzical look. "Medieval war novels," she explained. "She keeps slipping in deviations from historical facts. She's hoping he'll bolt up and call her on it."

"I don't know if that's sweet or sad. What's the prognosis?"

"The swelling's gone down. So far, no obvious signs of long term damage, but with the brain it's hard to say. At least that's what they tell me."

~ ~ ~

For the hell of it, Peter read the fifth Harry Potter book, *The Order of the Phoenix*. He decided Cho Chang was a twit and told Brent so.

~ ~ ~

Tuesday, June 7

Terry's eyelashes fluttered. Donna's heart stopped. Frantic, she ran to the nurses station and demanded a doctor. By the time one arrived, Terry's eyes were open and he was talking.

"Sir," the resident asked, "Can you tell me what year it is?"

"Gregorian, Julian, Mayan, or Jewish?"

Confused, the resident doggedly continued. "Sir, can you name the president?"

"You mean that fellow who let a serial killer babysit his children?"

The neurological resident looked bewildered. "Sounds delirious," he muttered to the nurse. "Sir, can you give me a name?"

"Comrade Urkel? How about asking me something worth answering, like the Pharaohs of the 19th Dynasty, in order?" Tears ran down Donna's face. "Now, that was a government worth talking about. Ramses I, Seti I, Ramses II, Merneptah, Seti II, Amenmesse, Siptah, ah, and we must not forget little known and under-appreciated Queen Twosret." He punctuated the last name with a pointed index finger.

"Sir, you aren't making any sense."

"Only due to your limited intelligence. Fetch me a doctor with a real education."

The resident noticed Donna smiling through her tears and realized that she was not at all upset by his patient's behavior. "Is this typical?"

"Terry is never typical. But this is normal for him."

~ ~ ~

All wasn't normal. Terry could recite the periodic table. He could calculate pi to twenty decimal places in his head. This he chose to do instead of counting backwards from 100 by three, as requested by the doctor. He named all the prime numbers under 500. He could not remember falling, or even being on the roof. They told him it was expected to have some memory loss of the events preceding a concussion.

Terry was bothered. He suspected that somehow, he'd forgotten something important.

Chapter 18

Saturday, June 18

Bailey twitched the mosquito netting in place on their improvised butterfly house.

"It's a bit much, isn't it?" Lia asked, eyeing the plethora of hanging baskets full of Fuchsia and Tuberous Begonias. Pots of Geraniums in every color were stacked around the pavilion's support posts and along the perimeter of the tent.

"But it's made her so happy. Our Catherine loves overkill. The butterflies will certainly be entertained. They aren't native, but they will make a lovely splash of color, and she can decorate her deck with these after the party's over."

"I'm so impressed. You've got her being smug about her plants not being jammed in like sardines."

"It just took citing a few eco-conscious Hollywood types who've gone the native plant route, giving her a few names to drop. She now knows she's in exalted company."

"Lia! Bailey! Have I told you how wonderful this is?" Catherine picked her way across the stepping stones in her 'koi moat' to the little island. Lia watched her totter across the creek in her spike-heeled sandals and mentally shook her head. "How brilliant of you to come up with a canopy of mosquito netting so the butterflies would have sunshine. Is everything ready to let them loose?"

"Whenever you say," Lia responded. "We've placed extra pots of flowers for them to feed on while they're in here."

"It looks lovely! I thought about waiting until everyone was here later this evening, but then I thought, why keep them cooped up any longer? Their lives are so short, they should get all the sunshine they can."

"If you want, you can sit in the tent and open the hatchery. You'll get to watch them come out, and you can spend some time alone with them."

"What a marvelous way to get ready for the party!"

Lia pulled the hatchery out from under the bench. "We'll leave you, then. Just be sure to close the netting all the way when you come out." She showed Catherine the strips of magnets designed to ensure the flaps sealed securely.

They left Catherine to enjoy her island paradise and strolled the path, savoring bright splashes of blossoms. "It turned out well, didn't it, Bailey?"

"I'd say so. Maybe some of Catherine's society friends will want one of their very own."

"You going to be okay now?"

Bailey sighed, "For a while I was wondering if I was going to be able to see it through. Thanks for running interference."

"Hey, what are friends for? I could wait awhile before we tackle another one. I swear, I'll never agree to such an insane schedule on a big job again."

"It's like childbirth. They tell me you forget all the pain and that's the only reason anyone ever does it again."

"Yeah, you're right. I get in the middle of some huge project and I promise myself I'm never going to do it again and then I turn around and make a proposal for something twice as big. Come on, girlfriend, let's go put on our party shoes."

~ ~ ~

"Detective, Officer, I'm so glad you both made it." Catherine's smile was bright and impersonal as she ushered Peter and Brent into her side yard. "Have you seen the labyrinth? You *must* walk it. There's food and drinks by the back deck. Don't forget the sushi bar." She wafted off, the lavender and cerise silk of her caftan fluttering behind her. Peter suspected she had decided to take the butterfly theme to heart.

He heard strains of exotic music pulsing from the rear of the property. "What is that?" Peter asked.

"I think it's called Ethno-trance-fusion or something like that. Sounds like Mayan Ruins. Gotta love those drums, they're positively tribal," Brent said. "You go check out the labyrinth, I'm looking for a beer."

Peter followed the winding path into Lia's garden. He let jewel-toned mosaics lead him through the loops and turns. His mind wandered with his feet and he thought about the woman who could create such loveliness, for whom looking at the world around her was an adventure and a delight. He wondered what she saw in him, an ordinary guy with no special window on the world. One more turn brought him to the edge of the koi pond . . . no, koi *moat,* as Lia told him Catherine insisted on calling it. Brightly colored fish darted among rocks and aquatic plants. He looked up and saw Lia sitting on the bench, still as a statue while Painted Ladies and Swallowtails floated around her on dancing wings. He crossed the moat.

"I'd knock, but there's nothing to knock on," he announced.

"Come on in. I saw you on the path. Did you enjoy the walk?"

"Not as much as I'm enjoying myself now." He could swear the air around her sparkled as she smiled. "Is there room on the bench for two?"

"I suspect so." She scooted to one side. If you're quiet, they may land on you."

"Really?"

"Three of them have sat on me so far."

"That's because you smell so pretty."

"That's because I didn't have you here for competition. Just sit still and wait. Don't talk."

He wrapped an arm around her and she dropped her head against his shoulder. He imagined himself sitting with her, just like this, no butterflies necessary, when he was old and arthritic. Just Lia leaning on his shoulder, maybe looking at a fire, or watching a sunset. It was a warm thought. A Painted Lady fluttered down and sat on his shoulder. Lia grinned at him and he leaned over to kiss her, a brush of lips as soft as butterfly wings.

"Aw. She flew off," Lia pouted.

"That's okay. I got a grip on the prettiest lady here. I don't need any others."

"You're sweet."

"On you."

"Really?"

"Really."

"Hmmm," Lia considered.

"You can't be surprised."

"Guess not. You're not exactly the Sphinx."

"What do we do about this?"

Lia gave a contented sigh. "This is nice, just like this."

"Yes, it is."

"I really like you, Peter. You're so solid. And I feel like you really see me. I just don't want to jump in and fall flat on my face. After Luthor I'm having a hard time trusting myself, my judgement. But this is really nice. I don't think I've ever felt so comfortable with anyone before, just being, you know?"

"I think I do." He gave her a squeeze. "Shall we go find some food? Patronize the famous sushi bar? Discover what other delicacies are in store for us?"

"Might as well. After all the agony Catherine's put us through, Bailey and I better get our money's worth tonight."

"I can't believe what you and Bailey accomplished, it's amazing. I hope I get to see it when the plants are established. You did a really great job." He used the excuse of the stepping stones to hold her hand, then kept it after they crossed the water.

They stopped by the sushi station, where the chef was slicing a California Roll for Brent. "So this is the lovely Lia. How'd you get mixed up with this clown?"

Lia gave Brent a flirtatious look. "It's the itty-bitty car and the big red nose. Gets me every time. I can't help myself. Are you having a good time?"

"Nice party. I've met a few of your friends. Some guy named Terry in a wheelchair. Is he for real?"

"'Fraid so," Lia and Peter said in unison.

"He said he was helping you find a gun. Said something about how he thought he remembered seeing it before, but it turned out it was only some weird brand of air pistol."

Peter shook his head. "Barely out of the hospital, and he's already back on the case."

"Bailey was suggesting that she bring in some of her mystical friends and have a seance to get Luthor to tell us where he got the gun, then Terry went off on a riff about 19th Century table-tipping fraud. He offered to be in charge of manufacturing her special effects."

"Glad to hear his accident didn't slow him down any."

"Peter!" Lia scolded.

Nadine rounded a bush and spotted Lia. "Lia, have you seen Catherine?" she asked, distractedly.

"Not recently. What's wrong?"

"It's Marie and Terry. They're at it again."

"Surely not."

"Surely yes."

"How are Catherine's other guests taking it?"

"They're appalled, of course. Charlie's been looking for Catherine, but I don't think he's found her yet. I've got to put a stop to this somehow. It's just not right, it's a party, for Heaven's sake." She stalked off towards the band, shaking her head and muttering to herself.

Peter frowned, mentally gearing-up into cop-mode. Lia saw his face, read his mind. "Sorry, Detective, you may be the long arm of the law, but there's not a thing you can do." She gave him an appraising look and sighed, " I suppose you'll have to see for yourself."

She took him by the hand and led him around to the crowded deck. They pushed through to the center. Terry sat in his wheelchair, facing off with Marie. Terry's eyes were predatory slits behind his wire-rim glasses. Marie's head was canted to a dangerous angle, her eyes narrowed, her magenta bangs a bold stroke of defiance. Catherine's other guests were slack-jawed and gaping.

Marie spoke first, "Sarah Palin filed a complaint of sexual harassment against Dick Cheney for talking about her enormous rack."

"Oh, really?"

"But it didn't go anywhere. Turns out he was talking about the antlers on the last moose she bagged."

Terry grunted in a mild acknowledgment of the hit. He leaned forward and gripped the arm rests of his wheel chair.

"In the Eighties, when Ronald Reagan was president, Bob Hope and Johnny Cash were still alive. Now we've got Obama, no Hope and no Cash."

Marie snorted derisively. "Why didn't Sarah Palin cross the road?"

Terry rolled his eyes in an attempt to display boredom. "Gee, I don't know. Why?"

"She had a new laser-scope and it wasn't necessary."

"What will we have when they put Obama's face on a quarter?"

"I don't know. What?"

"Finally, 'Change you can believe in.'"

"Why did Sarah Palin bleach her hair?"

"No idea."

"It was time to shoot dinner and it was snowing outside."

Donna sidled up to Lia and Peter. "They have an audience. I don't think there's any stopping them."

A rail-thin, cultured blond leaned over. "How long will they keep this up? This is unbelievable!"

"It could be hours," Donna moaned.

The blond shook her head. "It's like a train wreck. I can't help watching."

"Fascinating, isn't it?" Lia asked.

"Yes, in a very weird, sick way," the blond said, shaking her head.

"They score points, you know," Donna added.

"Seriously?"

"They can't repeat a joke and the one who runs out first has to buy at the next Burger-Mania lunch. Right now, I think Marie is winning."

"And what do you get for putting up with it?"

Donna smiled, "I get Terry."

Just then, the music stopped. After a moment of dead silence, a single drum started the familiar rhythm of the Conga. The sound got louder, as if it was moving closer. A tambourine joined in, then a cowbell. Slowly the crowd parted. Paul Ravenscraft, the band's bearded drummer, appeared carrying a djembe in an improvised parade harness as he rapped out the syncopated siren song. Nadine clung to the waist strap of his harness with one hand while she shook the tambourine with the other. She waved the noise-maker at Lia and Peter in a "come on down" gesture. Catherine gyrated behind Nadine with the cowbell, giving an extra twist to her hips on the downbeat. Jose, Bailey and Brent were behind her. Brent gave a "what the heck" shrug as he shuffled with the beat. The Conga line snaked through the crowd, picking up dancers as it moved along.

Lia grabbed Peter's hand and pulled him towards the expanding train of party guests.

"Must we?"

"You'd rather listen to bad Obama jokes?"

"Good point." He joined the line behind Lia, settling his hands on her hips. He decided this was much better than questionable political humor. The line circled the garden, then took a serpentine path around the house. The crowd around Marie and Terry dissipated, absorbed into the dance. Lia looked back at the deck. Terry was good-naturedly banging on the cowbell while Donna pushed his wheelchair around the deck in time with the music.

The line began to zig-zag across the flagstone patio, filling up the make-shift dance floor. Paul rejoined his bandmates as other instruments started to play. The band segued into the softly pulsating rhythm of an original tune. Lia turned around, into Peter's arms.

Peter froze. "You know, Kentucky boys can't dance."

"Do Kentucky boys keep time?"

"That we do."

"What if we just stay like this and keep time? You just have to sway a little. It's so crowded, nobody will notice us anyway." She wrapped her arms around his neck and looked into his eyes. Peter thought maybe Kentucky boys did dance, just a little.

Peter left Lia surrounded by high-maintenance women from Hyde Park and Amberly Village. It was all in the fingernails, he thought. He found fake fingernails a repellent reminder that some people had more money than sense. Money enough, perhaps, to commission a garden of their own? He figured the cooing was a girl thing and headed over to the bar for a beer, promising to bring a mohito for Lia. He pried Bailey away from Anna and sent her back with the mohito. As long as there was cooing, she might as well get some. Better her than him.

He found Brent, Jim, and Jose talking to a bear of a man who was Catherine's husband, Leo. Leo was a Steelers fan, in opposition to 90% of Cincinnati. He stated that only the brain-dead held to home-town loyalties in the face of superior skills and a solid winning record. Jim replied that true love is unconditional. Brent said he didn't care too much one way or the other, as long as he didn't have to go around calling himself a 'Cheesehead,' which was the fate of Cincinnatians who chose Wisconsin over Pittsburgh in the last Superbowl. Jose thought this was funnier than it deserved to be. When Leo asked what his game was, Peter suggested that baseball was a real thinking man's sport and turned the conversation to the Red's current season, the Reds being much easier to love than the Bengals.

179

He was sitting on the deck steps, enjoying the star-lit sky when he felt a hand on his shoulder. "There are severe penalties for deserters," Lia announced, mock-stern.

"How can I be a deserter when I sent you reinforcements and a mohito?"

"With that crowd, I needed tequila shots. Flaming tequila shots."

"I thought they were fans?"

She sat down beside him, placed a hand companionably on his knee. "They were nice enough. Socialites aren't my usual cup of tea, but I can stand it when they're talking about how wonderful a customized garden sculpture would look in their yard."

"So do you think you'll get some future business from this?"

"We'll see who's actually willing to buy. I especially liked Renee. She says she wants something designed to mark the solstice and equinox points, some kind of mosaic, Stone Henge-y thing. I think that's mostly to out-do Catherine."

Peter affected a huge sigh. "So young to be so suspicious."

"Hah. Says the man who wouldn't stick around to listen to it. But maybe one of them will come through. That or maybe someone will get a jones after they see it during the annual garden tour next month. It was nice of you to send Bailey over."

"I just figured you might like some back-up."

"It made it easy for me to make sure she got her share of the credit. And I think she's going to get some landscaping work out of it. So thank you."

Peter shrugged, took a pull on his beer. "No biggie."

"So how are you enjoying the party?"

"It's been nice. I met Leo."

"He's a force to be reckoned with, isn't he?"

"He's something. Brent and Jose seemed to have hit it off." He looked down and found Lia's hand in his.

"Really?" Lia's raised eyebrow mirrored Peter's own disbelief at this odd combination.

"Kid you not. Mr. Atlanta Metrosexual meets the West Side's Slider champ."

She shook her head. "How will they ever find a bar where they both can drink?"

"One of life's great mysteries. They may have to settle for Bar-B-Que and ice tea. Terry's been giving astronomy lectures." He gestured with his long-neck. "That big W up there is Cassie-something-or-other."

"Cassiopeia. The queen so vain the gods decided to punish her by giving her daughter to a sea monster."

"That doesn't seem fair."

"Greek gods are not big on fair. So what did you have planned for the rest of the evening?" She gave his hand a little squeeze.

Peter contemplated this question while he took a pull on his beer. "My dance card appears to have a few vacant spots on it."

"Not surprising, since you don't dance. What say I say my good-byes and you say your good-byes and you swing by my place? We can see about filling those spots on your dance card."

"Sounds fair to me."

Lia stood up, tugged on his hand and pulled him up. "Ain't nothin' fair about it, Kentucky Boy."

Chapter 19

Peter rolled over and snagged his phone off the bed-side table. He froze for a moment, confused by a fringed, amber lampshade. Slivers of daylight revealed unfamiliar slashes of color. He shook his head, remembered where he was, and smiled. Then he looked at the screen. Groaned. Dispatch. The time was 6:43 a.m. Shit. Thank God he only had a few beers last night. A hangover after less than 5 hours sleep would be murder. He sat up and flipped the phone open. "Dourson."

"Detective, we have a suspicious death at 843 Hosta Terrace. You flagged that address on one of your cases. I know this is your day off, but I thought you would want the call."

"Thanks. Who's the deceased?"

"Her name is Catherine Laroux."

"I'll be right there." He rolled over and looked at Lia. Should he tell her? What a way to spoil the mood. Not yet. She'd find out soon enough. He stroked her hair.

"Mmmph."

"I gotta go."

"Do you have to?" she murmured, half asleep.

He nuzzled her neck. "Yeah. Work." Nipped her earlobe.

She turned her face so that their lips met. "See you later, Kentucky Boy," she breathed into his mouth.

By the time Peter was dressed, Lia had fallen back asleep. So much for romance, he thought, and kissed her on the back of her head as he left.

Peter winced when he saw crime scene investigators tromping all over the labyrinth. He ducked under the yellow tape, flashing his badge at the officer posted there, and was directed to the center of the maze. He sighed as he saw the path, established by other officers, cutting straight through the garden. He knew he couldn't walk Lia's mosaic path because it might contaminate evidence, but he regretted the damage to the plants. Then it occurred to him that he was more concerned about the garden than he was about Catherine. Maybe because he never met a flower who would sleep with its friend's boyfriend, if flowers had boyfriends, which they probably didn't, seeing as how pollen was delivered by bees. Kinda like getting sperm in the mail. A depressing thought which explained why all the flowers got along and gardens were such peaceful places. Nothing to fight over.

He spotted Catherine lying in the mulch at the edge of her koi moat, her silk caftan soaked and crumpled up around her legs, her halo of dandelion-fluff hair sodden and lank. Brent was already there, talking to Dr. Jefferson. "Amanda, Brent," he nodded, "What have we got?"

Amanda Jefferson was a sturdy black woman sporting a heavy mop of braids down her back. She stood up from where she had been kneeling by the body. "Can't say for sure until the autopsy, but it looks like a - no pun intended - garden variety drowning." Gardener showed up shortly after sunrise, found her floating in the pond here and hauled her out, then called us."

"Bailey? Bailey's here? Where is she?"

Brent pointed back towards the house. "She's on the deck. She's really upset."

"I imagine so. Do we have any idea about time of death?"

"Hard to say. I'll have to account for the cold water. Several hours, though. We've got rigor mortis setting in. Brent said she threw a party last night."

"Yeah, we were both here."

Amanda raised an eyebrow. "Undercover work?"

"Nah. Mostly Mrs. Laroux was showing us what a generous and forgiving person she was after Peter and I grilled her like tuna a few weeks ago. Looks like she never made it to bed. These are the same clothes she had on last night. Why do we think this might not be an accident?"

"Pond's less than three feet deep. Hard to drown when all you need to do is sit up. There's a contusion on the side of her head. Difficult to say right now if someone hit her or if she hit it on one of those rocks." Dr. Jefferson pointed to the stepping stones. "There are no defensive wounds. No obvious sign of a struggle. We'll run tox screens. If she was drunk, that would explain it."

"She seem drunk to you, Brent?"

"Not when I left. Doesn't mean she didn't have a few after everyone was gone. Shall we find Bailey and see what she says?"

Bailey was hunched up in a saffron-colored Adirondack chair, staring at nothing. Peter and Brent pulled up chairs and sat across from her.

"Bailey, I'm so sorry."

"Peter, I don't understand. First Luthor, then Terry, now this."

"I know it's hard, but we need to ask you some questions. Do you remember Officer Davis?"

"We met last night."

"Bailey, can I get you something?" Brent offered. "Water? Coffee?"

"Nothing. I don't think I can stomach anything right now."

Peter pulled out his recorder. I'd like to tape this for accuracy's sake, if that's all right with you."

Bailey nodded her assent. "Am I a suspect or something?"

"Right now we don't know if there's been a crime. That's what we're trying to figure out. Can you state your name for the record?

"Hughes, Bailey Hughes." She chewed on a thumbnail and looked past him.

"What time did you arrive this morning?"

"I got here just before six."

"What brought you out here today?"

"Catherine figured there might be some damage to the plants with everyone wandering around last night. I agreed to check it out first thing today."

"And was there?"

"Not then. Not until you guys got here." Her tone was flat. Her expression as she surveyed the officers combing the garden, was wooden.

Peter winced. "Sorry about that. How did you find Mrs. Laroux?"

Bailey took a deep breath, and brushed her hair out of her eyes. "I was walking the path, checking everything out. Halfway in, the path runs along the pond for a bit. I saw this lump in the water by the stepping stones. I was getting pissed and wondering what it was and then I saw her hand, floating there. I ran over and pulled her out. I was going to do CPR, but she was cold and stiff. I called 911."

"Do you remember how her body was laying?"

"She was to the right of the stepping stones."

"Face up or face down?"

"Face down."

"And were her feet towards the island, or away?"

"Away. Does this matter?"

"We don't know yet. It's a good idea to get as much information as possible while it's still fresh in your mind. Was anything disturbed, that you noticed?"

"I didn't notice much of anything after I saw Catherine."

"When was the last time you talked to her?"

"Around 10:30? That's when I left."

"Did you notice anything unusual then? Anyone acting strange at the party?"

"Like what?"

"Anyone acting unhappy, any tension, anything out of the ordinary?"

"Catherine was just Catherine. It was a nice party. Nothing odd."

"Can we call anyone for you? Lia, maybe?"

"Lia's going to freak. Catherine dead, the garden trashed."

Lia was brave when Peter called her. He had a uniform stay with Bailey until she arrived.

Leo sat at his kitchen table, clenching a mug of coffee like a lifeline. Last night the large man seemed imperious and imposing. Morning light etched grief into his face. Peter walked him through the usual questions.

"What was her mood last night?"

"She was happy. Catherine loves parties. I hate them."

"When was the last time you saw her?"

"I went to bed around 11:30. She still had some late guests."

"You didn't notice when she didn't come upstairs?"

"No, I didn't notice. I have sleep apnea. We have separate bedrooms so I don't disturb her." Leo began to sound testy.

"Can you recall who was still here at that time?"

"That Asian woman with the pink hair. Some of her literary friends. I don't know their names." Peter wrote "Marie Woo" in his notebook and underlined it.

"Can you think of anyone who might want to hurt her?"

"Are you saying someone did this to her? I thought she slipped."

"We don't know. She might have. Right now there's no indication anyone else was involved. We're just trying to cover all possibilities."

Leo grimaced. "Catherine was a vain woman, and often silly. But I can't think of anyone who hated her, not like that."

Peter hated to do it, but he didn't have a choice. "Were you aware, Mr. Laroux, that your wife had an affair several months ago?"

Leo exhaled heavily. He looked sideways and worked his mouth angrily. "My wife had her hobbies. Yes, I knew. I also knew it was over."

"How did you know that?"

"He wasn't her first. Every time one ends, she gets on some kick. Has to remodel the house or something. This time it was those silly dogs and that garden."

"Did that upset you?"

"What do my wife's affairs have to do with anything?"

Peter and Brent looked at him steadily. Peter said quietly, "That man is dead. Now your wife is dead. Strange, don't you think? You ever meet Luthor Morrisey?"

"Was that his name? We've been married a long time. Our lives were often separate. I don't know half the people Catherine associated with."

"So you didn't care?"

"Of course I cared!" Leo exploded. "I loved her. But we both had our faults."

Peter and Brent finished with Laroux and walked back out to the deck. Lia had arrived and was sitting next to Bailey, holding her hand. She looked up at Peter, tears in her eyes.

"Poor Catherine. We barely finished the garden. She had less than a week with it, now she's dead. I can't believe it. She'll never get to see it in full bloom. And now people are stomping all over it. It's like they're stomping all over her."

"I'm so sorry," Peter said helplessly.

Peter studied the two officers combing the garden for evidence. One of them, Officer Hinkle, spotted Peter and stopped what he was doing to pick up an evidence bag. He headed over to the group on the porch. Lia looked up as the young man arrived. She had a bemused expression on her face. "Where did you get my phone?"

Stunned, Peter asked, "How do you know that's yours?"

"See the thumbprint? It's paint. Alizarin Crimson. I did that."

Peter looked at Hinkle expectantly. "Officer?"

"It was in her pocket. The M.E. found it."

"What was Catherine doing with my phone?" Panicky, Lia tried to connect the dots. "Catherine? Why would Catherine have it? How could she have found it? Why wouldn't she have returned it to me?"

"Maybe she didn't find it," Peter said gently.

"But . . . you think she had it all along?. . . *She* had it?. . . Why? . . . Why would she have it? . . . Unless . . . *She* called Luthor? . . . *Catherine*? . . . How could Catherine do that? Why would Catherine do that?" Lia pleaded. "Why would she shoot Luthor?"

"We don't know that she did. They just found it. We don't know what it means yet."

Leo came outside in response to Lia's rising voice. "What are you saying, my wife shot someone? How can you say such a thing!"

"Please, sir," Brent interjected, "Something has turned up that may be connected to a suspected homicide. We don't know yet why Catherine had it in her possession."

"Does this have to do with that sleeze, Morrisey, my wife was sneaking around with?"

"What?" Lia and Bailey cried out simultaneously.

Lia stared first at Leo, then at Peter. Her eyes widened. "You *knew*! I can see it in your face! You knew and you didn't tell me! How could you lie to me like that?"

"Lia, please, I couldn't tell you."

Bailey struggled to catch up. "Luthor was murdered?"

In the end, Brent drove a stony-faced Lia and a flabbergasted Bailey home. He caught up with Peter back at District Five. "I don't know, Bro. This is way past Chang and Potter. I don't think J.K. Rowling ever dealt with anything like this."

"Brilliant. Think she'll ever forgive me?"

"Hard to say. Not like you could tell her. Maybe she'll figure that out. You're a cop, the job has to come first when it's something like this."

Chapter 20

Sunday, June 26

She didn't figure it out. A week later, she still hadn't returned any of his calls. Meanwhile, the medical examiner's report on Catherine was inconclusive. Minimal alcohol in her system, no defensive wounds, and nothing about the wound on her head to determine whether someone hit her or she fell on a rock. Nothing to suggest why she had a smoking gun in her pocket.

Late party goers had left en mass at midnight. Some remembered Catherine saying she might walk the labyrinth after everyone was gone, since the moon was so bright. Peter was flummoxed by Lia's phone. What was Catherine doing with it? Was she going to hide it in the garden? That would be dangerous, with Bailey still digging around. And why hide it then? Maybe she just wanted to take it out and gloat, in her special place. Had Catherine fooled them all with her society floozy act? It was unsettling to think his instincts had been so far off.

Leo Laroux quietly took possession of his wife's body, had it cremated, and scattered the ashes in the garden. He just as quietly put the house up for sale, not wanting to live with the gossip about his now notorious wife.

And Lia still didn't call.

"I don't know," he told Alma. "I know she's been through a lot, but this is too much like work." They were in Alma's small back-yard greenhouse, repotting her overabundance of root-bound Aloe Vera plants.

Alma was a bird-like woman with an efficient cap of hair that remained stubbornly black on her aging head. She gave him a sympathetic pat and two of the plants for his apartment. "Won't do anything for a broken heart, but they're great to have around for burns. You and that girl have had nothing but bad timing. It'll sort itself out, it always does. Wouldn't hurt you to keep practicing that 'sorry' look, though."

Viola looked at him with liquid brown eyes, as if she knew what was troubling him. She'd taken to laying her head on his thigh while he sat on his couch and watched television. She appeared to agree with him as he pointed out technical errors on cop shows, twitching her expressive brow in concentration. He found himself talking to her about Lia. She never answered, but she seemed to understand. "We'll give it some time," he told her. "Not a good idea to go to the park now." She gave him a morose lick and submitted to leashed walks around the neighborhood.

~ ~ ~

Lia listened to the message for the fourth time. "Lia, please call me. Give me a chance to explain. Viola and I miss you." Low blow, bringing Viola into it. Her finger hovered over the delete button, but she couldn't bring herself to lower it the inch necessary to erase his voice.

"I do *not* need another man keeping secrets from me," she told Honey. She turned to Chewy. "Don't look at me like that. I know you're on his side. Men always stick together. Jerks. You need to remember where your kibble comes from, young man."

Geezlepete, she needed to get a grip. She turned to her latest canvas, dug into her paint box. The ritual of setting up her palette soothed her. This was her second painting of the cactus. The bloom had faded weeks ago, so she was painting the succulent green body of the plant. She wanted this one to pack a punch. It struck her as ironic that she felt the need to create something confrontational when she was avoiding Peter. Perhaps this was why she was ducking him. She was too stirred up, too angry, and not sure exactly what she was angry about. Not that there wasn't plenty to piss her off. But her feelings hadn't taken form yet.

During her last session, she painted the body of the plant. Today she would paint the spines. She took a liner, a slim brush with exceptionally long bristles, and dipped into her linseed oil, then some Naples Yellow. As she drew the spines on the plant, she felt them, like pricks to her heart. She began to name them in her head. 'Here's Luthor calling me a cunt. Here's finding out he wasn't broke. Here's being told he had other women. Here's discovering Catherine slept with him. Here's working for that bitch while I didn't know about her and Luthor. Here's realizing that Peter knew about it for weeks and kept it from me. Here's feeling like a fool.'

The spines weren't sharp enough, dangerous enough, hard enough. She started shading one side with a hairline of purple as she continued her litany. 'Here's thinking Peter was different. Here's believing I was falling in love with him. Here's finding out I can't trust him, that I can't trust any man.' The pain in her gut was sharp, like knives. She sat down on the floor with the brush still in her hand, hugged her knees, and howled.

~ ~ ~

Wednesday, July 7

It was July when he decided to go back to the park. "My man," Terry called to him. "We thought you and the lovely Viola were lost to us forever." Terry was cheerful, despite casts on both legs. His wheelchair was parked by a picnic table as he held court with Jose and Charlie in attendance.

"I thought maybe I was persona non-grata," Peter admitted.

"An unacceptable person? Stick with us lads, we'll provide sanctuary from hostile entities."

"Thanks. And are there hostile entities?"

"Indeed. Indeed there are. The female contingency is dangerous right now."

"Yeah, I figured."

"Don't worry," Jose winked and flexed his muscles. "We'll protect ya."

"Gee," Peter commented dryly, "thanks."

"We haven't seen you since the party," Charlie commented. "Is it true what they're saying? Did Catherine really shoot Luthor? I find that hard to believe."

"So do I. But someone stole Lia's phone and used it to lure Luthor here that night, and Catherine had it. What other explanation is there?"

Jose shook his head. "You think you know someone. She could be a pain, but I never woulda thought she'd kill somebody."

"Spooky," Charlie said.

"Seems strange," Terry added. "She was always the decorative female. Hard to conceive of her as competent and soulless enough to plan and execute murder. Did you find out where the gun came from?"

"Nope. I don't think we ever will."

"I thought I had it solved. I saw a gun years ago and I thought it might be the same one, but she said hers had been a Schimel air pistol, not a Luger. I understand the two are virtually identical to casual inspection. Easy mistake to make. I thought maybe Luthor had lifted it, but she tells me she packed it away and it's been in the attic since before she knew him. If it was Catherine, that would be even less likely. Moot point, since it's not the right gun, anyway.

"Sounds like a dead end." Peter, half-listening, responded. He watched Viola chase Napa in circles around them. Charlie's lab, Oggie, was playing tug-of-war with Jose's Sophie. At least the dogs were having fun.

Chapter 21

Saturday, July 9

Lia watched the shifting pattern of leaves cast on the ground by the tree overhead and was grateful for the shade. It was before 8:00 a.m. and the sun was already cranking up. Now if only people would mind their own business. She felt guilty at that thought and glanced at Anna seated next to her on the picnic table. Anna was watching CarGo thrash in a child's wading pool. Someone had brought it to the park and left it by the water pump. Anna sensed the attention and turned to her.

"Lia, are you sure you're being reasonable?" Anna queried. "Why don't you talk to him?"

"How am I not being reasonable? How can I talk to him? He made a fool out of me. I slept with him, and he knew the woman I was working for slept with Luthor, maybe even *killed* him. He knew and he didn't tell me. I've *never* felt so humiliated."

"But how could he tell you? He's like a priest, some things he has to keep secret."

"All that time we were building the garden and feeling sorry for her because she was such a twit, and here she . . . she . . . *cuckolded* me! And then she stole my phone and shot

Luthor. And my boyfriend was a cheat and a gigolo. I can't *stand* it! I'm giving up on men. Entirely."

"Oh, Lia, I'm so sorry. I can't imagine how you feel. But I can't believe Peter had any choice."

"Well, he shouldn't have slept with me."

"As I recall, you told me you moved on him, and you were crying at the time."

"Yeah. So what?"

"What man was ever rational around a crying woman, especially one who's trying to take his clothes off?"

"It's still humiliating."

"Think about it. If he had told you, would you have finished the garden with Bailey?"

"Well, no, of course not. How could I?"

"That would have been a real shame, because it's beautiful. I know how much doing this project meant to you. And that's yours. No one can take that achievement away from you. But you would have denied it to yourself if you'd quit. So maybe he did you a favor by not telling you."

"Some favor," Lia grumbled.

"I know you're hurting, but maybe he's hurting, too."

"Must you always be so sensible?"

"He's a good man, Lia. Much better than Luthor."

"Don't you think I know that?"

"And circumstances have been difficult."

"I know, I know."

"Maybe you should give him a chance now that all this ugliness is over."

"I dunno. I don't know if I can. And what about Catherine?"

"What about her, dear?"

"I don't know how to feel. I know she was silly and we didn't always like her and I should hate her, but in her own way she was our friend. Or at least she meant to be. I can't understand why she'd shoot Luthor. It boggles my mind."

"Lia, darling, Catherine was a vain, air-headed, narcissistic woman who cared only for herself. She was nice to us when it suited her purposes. She's not worth agonizing over. And you're better off without Luthor. Really. She did you a favor when she shot him. He would have kept bleeding you emotionally forever."

"You don't know that, and that's cold."

"I'm just trying to get you to see that life is better now without them, if you'll let it be. Here you've had this delightful detective panting after you and if Luthor had been around not only would you have not met him; if you had met him, you'd have been unavailable. Can't you see Luthor's death for the gift it is? You're free of him. You have a chance to have a new relationship with a lovely man. Can't you be happy with that and let Catherine and Luthor go?"

Lia stared at Anna, appalled. "You think it's a *gift*?"

"Freedom from rude, selfish people is always a gift, don't you think?"

Lia's pulse jacked up and her mind raced. Was this Anna? This is just too strange, too coolly rational. Crazy. Calm, she told herself. I need to get away, get away and think. She took a deep breath. Exhaled. "Anna, perhaps you're right. Maybe I've been looking at this all wrong. Look, I'm going to take the kids for a walk in the woods. I'll talk to you later." She called Honey and Chewy, and headed for the trees and the trail that led down the hill. She walked, deliberately casual, though part of her wanted to run.

Chapter 22

Saturday, July 9, Continued

Peter couldn't get it off his mind. No matter how happy his captain was to have Morrisey's murder solved and Laroux ruled accidental, he kept coming back to what Bailey said: "First Luthor, then Terry, now this." Before Catherine surfaced, literally, with the phone, he'd been looking for someone smart enough to make a murder look like a suicide. Someone who maybe had done it before. What if Terry's accident and Catherine's death were all part of the same pattern, meant to look like something they weren't? Terry's accident could have been fatal. Catherine having the phone on her was too convenient. Terry'd been asking questions about the gun; could he have made someone nervous? But who? Terry talked to everyone about the gun so it could have been anyone.

And why target Catherine? Did she know something? Or was she just convenient? Did someone know about her affair with Morrisey? Plenty of people knew Catherine was going to be out in the garden that night. Was it a crime of opportunity? Was it even a crime? Was he hallucinating? He should just file it away and move on, but no matter how he worked it, he couldn't buy Catherine as being soulless enough to stage Luthor's death, or smart enough to pull it off without leaving a truck load of physical evidence. Catherine was an obvious kind of woman, and he doubted she had her bridge club fooled for one minute about what she did after their meetings.

Was he looking at one murder, or two murders and an attempt? And if so, how could he prove it? The only anomaly was the gun, and so far it had proved untraceable. Terry said something about a gun. He'd been preoccupied and it hadn't registered. Someone had a gun that looked like a Luger but it wasn't? He needed to check this with Terry. Did Terry require another look? Was his accident an attempt to divert suspicion that went wrong? Or just a coincidence?

Technically, the case was closed, but it felt about as closed as the busted driver's side door on his uncle's old Chevy. Maybe he could fit a quick trip to the park in before he went to work.

~ ~ ~

Lia sat on a fallen log at the bottom of the ravine. Chewy and Honey chased each other across the creek and through the trees. She listened as they traded insults with a pair of chittering squirrels safely taunting from a high perch. They gave up and ran off to sniff for deer. She looked up at the network of intertwining branches overhead, the layers of leaves, following the linear pattern limb by limb. The filtering sunlight had never failed to bring her peace. Today it wasn't working.

She tried some deep breathing. She'd never been much for yoga and meditation, but Bailey swore by it. How was it done? In for a count of four, hold for a count of four, out for a count of four, hold for a count of four. She kept it up for a few minutes. It made her dizzy. Her head was spinning, so she gave it up.

She just couldn't grasp Anna's attitude. Anna had always been one to take life as it came, but to be happy about Luthor being shot? That was inconceivable. And no matter what Anna said, she couldn't wrap her mind around Catherine shooting Luthor. She could see them having an affair. She didn't like it, loathed thinking about all the times Catherine flirted with Luthor and she brushed it off as meaningless. What did that say about her, that it was so easy to deny it then, and so easy to see it now?

She had to be the world's biggest chump. And, dammit, what was wrong with grieving, with taking time to feel? But what was she grieving, really? Was it Luthor, or was it the fact of their relationship? She had thought he was giving her the space she needed. Instead, he was using the extra time to run around on her. And if she took that a bit further, was that what made Luthor attractive to her? That he wasn't as demanding of her time and energy as other men had been? She felt like she was touching on an ugly truth about herself. Something about intimacy, and maybe about control. Maybe dating someone who was busy with other women allowed her to maintain control over her life. Luthor had always been someone she could never marry. Had that also been part of the attraction? Knowing the relationship could go no further? Did she really want intimacy? Maybe not, the way she kept shoving Peter away. Was that the problem with Peter, that he was actually available to her?

Geezlepete. All the whirling thoughts were making her more crazy. She remembered something Bailey mentioned, the Buddhist practice of mindfulness. How you open your senses and take in everything around you without having thoughts about it. Pure experience with no judgments. Just soak it all up like soaking in sunshine on the beach. She closed her eyes and listened to the wind in the trees, felt sun on her eyelids, and tried to let her thoughts run past her like a gurgling creek.

A twig snapped behind her, jolting her out of the meditation.

~ ~ ~

Peter opened the rear door of his Blazer. Before he could grab Viola's lead, she bolted for the trees. "Great." He looked around and spotted Jim and Fleece on the side of the hill. He called up, "What do I do now? I've got an escapee loose in the woods."

Jim trotted down to the fence. "You've got two choices. You can wait until she comes back on her own, or you can go after her."

"How long will it take for her to come back?"

"An hour, maybe two."

"I can't wait that long, but I don't know how to get through this mess."

"There's a path, I'll show you. Not many people use it anymore. Wait a minute while I come out." Jim ran back up the hill, through the corral and down to the parking lot. He led Peter down an overgrown trail. "You know, I'm having a hard time getting a handle on everything that's happened."

"How so?"

"Lia told me your serial killer theory, how you thought it was one of us. I guess it's true Catherine shot Luthor, since she had Lia's phone, but do you really think Catherine was a serial killer?"

Peter stepped over a log. "Hard to say. What are your thoughts about it?"

"Catherine was very social. You always knew when she was around, she was never one to hide in the corners. She always wanted company, and she was always looking for attention and fishing for compliments. She put a lot of energy into staying in shape, and she loved for people to notice it. Seems like a serial killer would need to fade into the background. I don't think Catherine knew how to go unnoticed, and it isn't like her to do something all by herself. I can't see her skulking around like someone would if they were sneaking up on people and killing them." He held a branch aside so Peter could pass.

"Can't see her shooting Luthor. He was always flattering to her, I noticed. Not in her nature to get rid of a handsome young man who paid her compliments. They're saying she gave him money and maybe she wanted revenge. I don't think the money would have mattered to her, and for her to want revenge, she'd have to admit she lost him. I don't know that her pride would let her go down that path, if you know what I mean. I think her answer would be to find a younger man, who was more handsome, and parade him in front of Luthor. Someone like that fellow you brought to her party. You can't prove anything to someone who's dead."

"Interesting thought."

"Besides. If she was going to kill anyone, I think it would be a woman. Cut out the competition."

"So who do you think it was?"

"Hard to say. Makes me nervous, thinking that someone here killed Luthor and then framed Catherine and killed her, too. Makes me wonder if any of us are safe."

~ ~ ~

Lia looked up to see Bailey scrambling down the path. "Hey, Bailey, where's Kita?"

"She's around here somewhere, what's up with you? I haven't seen you in ages."

"I was having myself a good think. Only it's not getting anywhere."

"What's the problem?"

"I don't know what to think about Anna. The way she was talking today, she sounds like a different person. I'm confused. She sounded really heartless."

"Really? What did she say?"

"She thinks I should be happy Luthor's dead and just get on with my life. Like it's a gift."

"Sounds harsh," Bailey admitted, "but would that really be so bad?"

"It just doesn't seem right to be happy about people dying. And she said such awful things about Catherine."

"We've all been saying awful things about Catherine for months."

"This was different. Inhuman. Like she was talking about a bug and it didn't matter if it got squashed."

"There's another way to look at this."

"What do you mean?"

"Now Catherine can start over and try again in the next life."

"Try again?"

"She pretty much screwed this one up. She either deliberately taunted you by commissioning us to build her garden, or else she was so self-involved, so clueless, she didn't understand how hurtful that would be. Either way, I can't imagine her seeing the light this time around. So maybe it was time she started over."

"I don't know, Bailey. How can drowning be okay?"

"Life and death are illusions. We all just pass to another plane of existence. She's in a better place now, where she can see her life here on Earth and understand how she affected the people around her. Maybe it was karma for Catherine to die like that after she killed Luthor."

Irked, Lia snapped back, "You think? And what about Luthor. Was it karma for him to die like that? With his brains all over his car? You didn't have to see that. I did."

"I'm sorry you saw that. I can't say what Luthor's karma was. But he wasn't doing anyone any good here."

"Anna said Catherine did me a favor when she shot Luthor."

"Maybe she did, if you can let it go."

"I don't understand how you can think that."

"As long as I've known you, you've found a reason to be miserable no matter what's going on. When you and Luthor were together, he made you crazy, when you broke up you felt guilty, when you took him back, you hated yourself. Now he's gone and you're feeling guilty again. Happiness is a choice. You can accept what life gives you, embrace your circumstances, or you can change things. But you just sit in your mess and obsess."

"That's brutal, Bailey. Have I really been that bad? Have I been that awful to be around?"

"I've been your friend the best way I know how. You're talented and funny and you have a lot to give. But you choose to be caught in this cycle, and nothing I or anyone else has said has made any difference. You disliked Catherine when she was alive, now she's dead and it's like you lost your best friend, even though she had an affair with Luthor. Luthor cheated on you, he was a total scum-bag. And you're still giving him space in your head after he's been gone for two months. He doesn't deserve it, and it does him no good. You're using him as a reason to be miserable, and to push Peter away.

I thought if Luthor was gone, you'd lighten up. But you seem determined to be unhappy, no matter what."

Lia stared hard at Bailey. There was something feral in Bailey's eyes, something she hadn't seen before. "Bailey, this doesn't sound like you. You're usually all 'love and light.'"

"Since when is putting something out of its misery not a loving thing to do?"

At Lia's shocked look, Bailey relented. "Don't take me so seriously. I'm just thinking out loud. I just want what's best for you, you know that, right?" She put her arm around Lia and gave her a squeeze.

"Yeah, sure."

"So what else is new? Jose tells me you got a gun. Is that true?"

"Yeah, I'm on a waiting list for the concealed-carry class."

"What brought that on?"

"Too much happening around here. It made me nervous."

"That's wild."

"Aren't you afraid? You dragged Catherine out of her pond, doesn't it stay with you?"

"Not really. What happens, happens. Fear isn't going to stop it, Fear just ruins everything else."

"Well, I feel better with a little protection, especially when I go walking alone in the woods."

"And I thought protection was something you got at the pharmacy."

Lia laughed, relieved to see her friend back to her usual self.

"What kind of gun did you get?"

"I went to see Terry and Donna a few days ago. Terry gave me this little two-shot derringer. He said I could give him a painting sometime, something for Donna. You should have heard him, telling me all about the history of derringers, how with the old ones, the bullets flew slow enough that you could see the bullet in midair. He said they flew about twenty-five miles an hour. Now they go twice as fast. Apparently now they have derringers fit with laser scopes for competition shooting. I didn't tell Terry, but I think that's pretty dumb, to put a laser scope on a gun that doesn't shoot straight."

"I've never seen a derringer, can I look at it?"

"Sure." Lia pulled the tiny gun out of her pocket. Bailey held out her hand and Lia gave it to her. "It's nothing special."

Bailey turned it over in her hand. "Aren't you concerned someone might take it away and use it on you?"

"Terry and I talked about that, about being ready to shoot if you pull your gun, not pulling it just to intimidate. He said people don't find derringers intimidating anyway, so you're better off shooting than waving it around."

"It's not very big at all, is it?" Bailey mused.

"No, I wanted something I could keep in a pocket. It only holds two bullets. And with a barrel this short, it's not accurate at any distance. That's probably why Terry was willing to let it go. If it won't take down a bull moose at fifty yards, I don't think he wants it."

Bailey turned it over. "Cute little thing, isn't it?"

"Funny, isn't it? I can't believe it has rosewood grips. Doesn't look like you could hurt anything with it. Never thought I'd own a gun. Times change, I guess."

"So are you going to start doing target practice?"

"I suppose I'll have to. I need to know how to use it."

Bailey held the gun in her lap. She looked in Lia's eyes. "I'm sorry if I came on too strong earlier. You know I love you, right?"

"Sure Bailey."

"I just hate seeing you so unhappy. I hate seeing anyone unhappy. It's a mission, you know? Eliminating pain and suffering."

"I've never seen you so serious."

"Sometimes the loving thing is the hard thing. Tell me Lia, if you had the chance, would you like a fresh start?"

"What do you mean?"

"A do-over. Just get off the merry-go-round and start again."

Lia looked down at her hands. "I haven't been that unhappy. Maybe lately I've been struggling, but..."

She heard the metallic click of the hammer at the same time as she felt the muzzle on the side of her head, pressing into her left temple. Time stopped. Lia froze. Horror gripped her. This was Bailey, her friend and partner, the woman who helped her pour 3,000 pounds of concrete. It made no sense.

Her world narrowed to the pressure of the derringer's barrel on her skin. Her mind went blank. Seconds passed while she fought the constriction in her chest and felt a single bead of sweat trickle down the side of her face. She pleaded, "What are you doing? Bailey, give it back to me!"

"I will in a minute. Hold still, I've got my finger on the trigger, you don't want me to flinch. It's a mission, like I said, getting rid of pain and unhappiness. This is the easiest way."

Baileys voice faded in and out as Lia struggled to grasp her situation. Her voice trembled, barely audible as she pushed past the paralysis in her chest. "You can't mean this. We're friends! Why would you do this? This isn't funny. Please give it back." Tears sprang from Lia's eyes.

"Keep your hands in your lap. If you so much as breathe, I'll pull the trigger."

"Please, Bailey, what do you want? Tell me what you want." Lia cried harder.

"I just want the world to be a better place. Can you honestly say the world isn't better without Luthor and Catherine?"

"N-n-no."

"That's right. Luthor was a bad person. He cheated on you. He lied and he used people. Catherine was mean-spirited and selfish. I don't think you're bad, but I do think you're desperately unhappy. You had a chance to change that and you didn't take it. So maybe you need a fresh start."

"Please don't do this."

"I envy you, really. There are so many times I'd have liked the chance to start over, but suicide is a sin."

"Isn't what you're doing a sin?"

"How can it be sinful to help someone move on without the stain of suicide on their soul? How can it be sinful to rid the world of self-generated misery?"

Lia grasped at a straw. "What about your karma?"

"Souls at the highest levels take on karmic burdens that ultimately serve enlightenment. Hitler was an ascended master who galvanized the world through his actions. Hitler served a higher purpose, and so do I."

"Please, let me go. I won't tell anyone. I don't want to die."

"I won't enjoy this. I will miss you."

"This is wrong, Bailey."

"It'll be okay. You'll see," Bailey soothed, Think of that wonderful place you're going, and it'll all be over before you know it."

"No . . . " Lia forced the word out past her paralysis, a whisper of denial.

"Think loving thoughts, Lia."

Lia was suddenly bowled over. A gunshot blasted. Someone screamed. Bailey was rolling on the ground, bleeding, being harried by two balls of fur, one black, one golden. Chewy scolded in his high-pitched bark. Lia found herself on the ground. She scrambled through last year's leaves, desperately searching for the gun on the ground around her log. She caught the glint of steel out of the corner of her eye and lunged for it, fumbling the derringer into her hands. She pointed it at Bailey, panting raggedly. "Honey, Viola, stay!" The dogs stilled, but kept up a menacing growl. Bailey crouched on the ground with her arms over her head, begging, "Don't shoot! Don't let them hurt me!"

Jim and Peter came crashing into the clearing. "My God, Lia," Peter shouted, "What are you doing?"

Chapter 23

Friday, July 22

The canvas of rich corals and greens was propped inside his screen door. The note read, "Dinner at 8? My place?" Peter smiled. The painting of the cactus flower reminded him of Lia, her guarded attitude and her vulnerability. Did she realize she'd given him a self-portrait? He carried it in and punched her number one-handed on his phone while Viola danced around him.

"Peter!"

"I got your very attractive invitation," he said as he held the painting against the wall, visualizing how it would look over the sofa. He rejected the spot, wanting a place where he would see it while he was sitting around.

"And?"

"Must I wait until eight?" He walked over to the opposite wall and propped it up on the book case, then bent down, ruffling Viola's fur. She licked his nose.

"What did you have in mind?"

"Depends. What are you going to feed me?"

"Liver."

"Ugh. Make it ten. Better yet, let me send over Viola instead. She *loves* liver."

"It would serve you right. It's a surprise."

"Promise it's not liver."

"I'm not making any promises, but you can bring dessert."

He followed a familiar, pulsing music and the scent of wood smoke to her backyard. Lia stood over the grill, poking at coals. Honey and Chewy were stationed nearby, tracking Lia's every move and drooling like Pavlov's dogs. Peter took a moment to enjoy Lia's fluid movements as she arranged a pair of baking potatoes and lowered the hood of the grill. Viola whimpered, straining at her leash. Lia turned at the sound.

"Hey, Detective Peter. Come in and have a beer."

"Hey, yourself." He opened the gate and unclipped Viola so she could join the other dogs, then set a bakery box down on the table. He grabbed a Grolsch swing-top from the ice chest and took a long pull while he studied Lia. He was feeling wary, but hopeful. She looked subdued and a bit tired. He noticed that instead of her usual T-shirt and paint smeared cut-offs, she wore a lavender tank top and purple paisley Bermuda shorts. Her hair was loose, and it curtained her face as she turned. "How have you been?"

"I'm doing better. This whole summer has been one bombshell after another. That business with Bailey was the worst, worse than finding Luthor, even."

"You didn't have to go to all this trouble."

She gave a wan smile, "Grilling's easy as it gets. Anyway, cooking is therapeutic. Hang on a minute while I pull some things out of the fridge."

"Need a hand? I've got two."

"Sure, why not?"

He followed her into the kitchen, which was warm and smelled of yeast. "Fresh bread?" He raised his eyebrows.

"Punching dough is very satisfying." She handed him a bowl of Romaine and tomato wedges topped with a blackish paste. Peter looked at it and wondered if this was a bad sign. "My therapist thinks baking bread is a good outlet for my aggressions. Almost as good as working clay, but I'm not set up for that."

"I didn't know you had a therapist."

She's new. Like I said, it's been a rough summer." She pulled a plate out of the fridge and gestured to the door. "Shall we have some eats?"

He eyed the bowl suspiciously. "I'm not one to look a gift meal in the mouth, but what is this stuff?"

"What it is, is delicious. That's tappenade. It's a puree of olives and spices. If you don't like it, you can give all of yours to me. But I never took you for a culinary coward."

"I'm not, normally, but this stuff resembles something that came up in my drain once."

She rolled her eyes, "Have a little faith, Dourson. Tell you what, I'll eat it first so you'll know it won't kill you."

"Thank you. That's a big load off my mind. Is that plate what I think it is?"

"Tuna sashimi. I know you like sushi."

"I didn't know you could make the raw fish stuff at home."

"You can with tuna. That's the safest fish for do-it-yourselfers. Appetizer first, then salad."

There was something intimate about sharing the plate of sashimi. Lia showed him how she liked it best, laying a piece of pickled ginger on top of a tender slice of fish, then rolling it up and using a fork to dip it into wasabi-spiced soy sauce. She demonstrated, then fed the first one to him. They saved the last 3 slices of tuna for the dogs. Chewy and Honey gulped theirs right down. Viola carefully laid hers on the grass and sniffed at it. Peter watched with amusement. "I guess my dog is a culinary coward, too." After eyeing the morsel a bit longer,

Viola licked at it, then eyed it again and suddenly snarfed it up. Chewy sighed disappointedly.

A timer beeped. "Bread's ready." Lia dashed into the kitchen and emerged a few minutes later with a steaming loaf on a breadboard. "We have to wait a little bit while it cools down."

"Must we?" Peter gave her a mournful look.

Lia laughed, "Yes, unless you want to hurt yourself. Here, try this." She held out a fork holding a smidgeon of the black paste.

"I thought you were going to try it first?"

"Dourson, Dourson," she shook her head. "Some things are all about trust. Do you trust me?"

"I don't know. You've been really angry at me. You could be setting me up." Might as well get it out there, he thought. "I'm sorry you found out about Catherine the way you did. I would have found a better way to tell you, once it was going to be public knowledge. Until then, I couldn't say anything."

"It's not your fault. I've worked it out every way I could think of, and I don't believe you could have done any different. If I had been paying attention, I would have realized something was going on between Luthor and Catherine. And you warned me there might be more women. I finally realized that underneath all the drama Luthor created, I really didn't care enough to notice. So I'm going to forget about them, and I hope you will, too."

"Really?"

"Really. Enough serious stuff. Now are you going to eat your sewer sludge like a good boy or am I going to have to send you home without your moo-cow?"

"We're having moo-cow?"

"Duh. Grill. Moo-cow. It should be obvious."

"I thought you might be feeding me something girly, like Portabella steaks or veggie burgers."

"Dourson, Dourson, Dourson," she sighed. "We are really going to have to work on your trust issues." She offered the fork again. This time he opened his mouth. "That's better," she cooed.

The rich flavor of olives and garlic burst over his tongue. "Wow. Intense. Tasty stuff."

She picked up a large, serrated knife and sliced a generous heel off the loaf. The whole wheat bread steamed as she slathered on softened butter. Rivulets of butter melted while she spread it. "Here, take a bite of this."

He closed his eyes and concentrated on the flavor while it dissolved in his mouth. "This is Heaven. What did I do to deserve it?"

"Not a thing. But we could both use a break. I've been thinking you don't want your filet to cook very long, so why don't we finish our salads before I put the meat to the fire?"

"Sounds like a plan." He ate every last bit of salad, just in case that would have any bearing on the quality of his steak.

Peter manned the grill as the sky began to darken. They ate in companionable silence. After the rare meat and fully dressed, grilled potato were safely in his belly, after they fed scraps to three eager dogs, he commented, "I never knew you were so carnivorous. Those were positively bloody. It doesn't quite fit with the carrot juice."

"I'm a girl of depth and complexity."

"I can see that. You know, I just realized where I heard that music before. Is it that same band? What was their name? Mayan something?"

"Mayan Ruins. I've got their CDs." It was full dark now, with a bright quarter moon rising above the trees. "Kentucky Boy, I think they might be playing our song."

"Do you think so?"

"Yes, I absolutely do."

He took her hand and led her out onto the grass and into his arms. They swayed gently to the sensual syncopation until the maracas shimmied and the drums kicked up tempo, until it became a throbbing in his blood. Peter stopped. He took Lia's face in both hands and leaned down to kiss her, gently at first, then sinking, sinking.

~ ~ ~

Peter raised himself on his elbows after the pounding of his heart subsided. He watched Lia's face in the moonlight coming through her bedroom window, then kissed her lightly on the nose. She scrunched it up at him and sighed. "You know," he said, "I was afraid I'd never get to do that with you again."

"That would have been a real shame."

"You know what's a real shame?"

"What?"

"Our dessert, sitting in the backyard, waiting for the raccoons to get it."

"Oh! I forgot all about it! Do you suppose it's still there?"

"Let me pull on my shorts and go check."

Lia grabbed a cotton robe and joined him out back on the stoop. The box was still intact. "What is it, anyway?"

"Open it up and see."

"It's dark."

"Here, I'll grab a fork and you'll just have to trust me this time."

"Sauce for the goose?"

"Something like that. Open wide."

The morsel was dark and creamy and bittersweet. "Oh, my God. Chocolate cheesecake. And dried cherries. This was sitting out here all this time and I didn't know it?"

Peter took a bite. "I hope you had better things to do."

"I don't know. This is pretty wicked."

"Now you're going to go and insult my prowess."

"Hey, Dourson?"

"Hey, what?"

"You dance just fine, Kentucky Boy. Now gimme another bite." She opened her mouth like a little bird and he obligingly fed her the rest of the slice. When it was gone, she examined him carefully. "I wasn't going to ask, but I think I'm gonna."

"Ask what?"

"Can you talk about Bailey?"

Peter thought. Yeah, some things really are about trust. "Probably not, but I will."

"Peter, I was never so scared. I froze. I was petrified. I just couldn't think, couldn't move. She had my own gun to my head. All I could do was cry and beg."

"I've never had a gun aimed at me. I can't imagine it."

"How did she figure she was going to get away with killing me?"

"She quit talking shortly after we took her into custody. First she was babbling nonsense and then she became non-responsive. They had to send her to a psych ward. She hasn't said a word in over a week. What we know is pieced together from interviews with other people and speculation.

"She knew you had the gun because Jose told her. Her truck was parked up at Maple Ridge Lodge. We figure she cut through the woods so no one at the park would see her. She left Kita at home. You take a lot of walks in the woods. I think she was looking for you down by the creek, and she probably planned to make it look like another suicide, like you were so distraught over Luthor that you decided to end it all. She factored everything in except the dogs."

The trio had been lolling on the grass. At the word "dogs," they perked their heads up. Peter laughed. "Yes, we're talking about you. Don't get big-headed on us."

"What's going to happen to her?"

"I know you were terrified, but I can't help wishing she'd talked just a little longer. You said she mentioned Catherine and Luthor. You're absolutely sure she never said she killed them?"

"From what I remember. Part of the time I was so freaked out, my ears stopped working. I couldn't hear a thing. I remember she said the world was better without them, and she said she had a mission to end pain and suffering. I don't remember her saying she killed anyone."

"Damn. We've got nothing to connect her to Catherine and Luthor. The crime scene folks have torn her house apart, looking for any connection to the gun, anything she might have kept as a souvenir. The IT folks are reviewing her computer to see if they can find any incriminating files. They're also reviewing her browser activity.

"She was visiting some very strange web-sites and forums, places that support that whole 'Hitler' thing you were telling me about. Her posts are frightening, you can see her coming apart. She hasn't admitted to anything about Luthor or Catherine, and if she's smart, when she comes back around she won't, since we have no physical evidence to implicate her. We're examining her life, looking for any possibility that she might have done it before.

"Right now, all we have is an attempted murder charge, and it'll be pled down to assault with a deadly weapon. She's getting a full psych evaluation. Her lawyer's insisting she never meant to pull the trigger, just to shock you, and that the gun went off accidentally because the dogs tackled her. Looks like she'll spend time in a psychiatric unit for violent offenders. I'm not happy about any of this. We need to put her away permanently, and we may not be able to do it."

"Do you think there's any chance that she didn't kill Luthor and Catherine, and that she really didn't mean to pull the trigger?"

"How big are the odds that you have two homicidal maniacs at the dog park?"

"Not very big, I guess. But Bailey! We've been friends for years. I still can't believe she'd try to kill me."

"If we're lucky, when the time comes she'll ignore her lawyer and and spill it all. Self-righteous types often do."

"It was so weird. She was acting so crazy. Still, there was a piece of what she was saying that really hit me, about choosing to be happy or unhappy."

"I don't think life is that black and white."

"No, it's not. But I sat on that log with a gun to my head and her finger on the trigger. She kept saying all this wild stuff about sending me to the other side. All I could think was, I'm going to die and I wasted all that time obsessing about that jerk, Luthor, and never gave you and me a chance." She turned to Peter. "Every time things got sticky, I pushed you away instead of dealing with it."

He put his arms around her and pulled her close. Their eyes met and held for a long moment, his searching, hers earnest. The world stilled while she waited for him to respond. Finally he gave her an odd half-smile and said, "Do you want to give me and you a chance?

"Yeah, I do."

"Really?"

"Really, Kentucky Boy."

"Sing me Viola's Pee song."
So she did.

Epilogue

Bailey was such a dupe. I so tired of listening to her nauseating New Age baloney. So delicious to turn it against her! Few people knew she was bi-polar. All I had to do was dump out the medication in her capsules and fill them with powdered aspirin to send her into a manic state. Then there were those two capsules I filled with a special chemical cocktail designed to push her over the edge. Easy enough to do since I knew where she hid her spare key.

A few suggestions of web sites touting a ridiculous theory about reincarnation, and Bailey became a woman with purpose. She'll never know I was the one responding to her posts on that forum, egging her on. Regrettable that she chose Lia as her first target, but I knew she didn't have it in her to pull the trigger. Foolish woman, trying to explain herself, as if she were going to get Lia's approval for her plan to send Lia out of this life and into the next one!

As much as they want to, they'll never connect Bailey to Luthor's murder. They'll either resign themselves that Catherine did it, or they'll have to let it go. The waters are sufficiently muddied and I am still under the radar.

I am fascinated by the new possibilities this event raises, achieving my aims through the manipulation of others. An elegant solution to the problem of establishing an alibi, as well as making it possible to remove more than one person from the same environment at the same time. Presuming the one manipulated is not as thorough as I am, they should get caught, eliminating themselves.

I am of two minds about this last round. On the one hand, I caved in to anxiety and broke my rules. It is questionable whether my actions after removing Luthor served a purpose. It is possible that had I just followed the rules and kept still, that everything would have been just fine. I could have disposed of the phone and no one would have ever connected me to Luthor, even if they suspected. But do I venture to say that this was invigorating? Even highly amusing? It was so satisfying to smash Catherine in the head with a rock! And the memory is so pleasurable. A clean, quiet removal has its rewards, but I was getting bored. Perhaps it's time to make the game more interesting.

I must consider this carefully, determine the ramifications. For now, all is well in my little world. I no longer have to endure Catherine and her narcissistic preening, Luthor and his drama, or Bailey and her mumbo-jumbo. Terry's going to be in casts for months, then physical therapy. That won't improve his political position, but at least when he's spouting off, I can look at his casts and remember booby-trapping his ladder. My mornings are pleasant again. And that's as it should be.

Viola's Song

You gotta circle to the left and
then you circle to the right
Sniff, sniff, sniff until it feels just right
Move along, do a little prance
That's Viola's dance

And so I circle to the left and then I circle right
And I sniff and I sniff, but nothing seems quite right
So I'll do it all again with a step that will entrance
That's Viola's dance

One more time!

Circle left, circle right
Sniff, sniff, oh boy, that's outta sight!
Do a little squat with a wiggle of my pants
That's Viola's dance

Ahhhh!

Author's Notes

There really is a Mount Airy Dog Park, and I've been taking my furry horde there almost daily for more than eight years (It has recently been renamed the Doris Day Dog Park). A few of the park regulars made it into the book under aliases (with their permission). Any truly heinous character is a product of my mind, and not to be confused with any real person. Terry Dunn is only slightly less intelligent in real life than he is in the book. Jose really is the nickname of an Italian guy whose family has called him Jose since he was a baby. Many of the dogs in the book exist. Mayan Ruins is a real (fabulous!) band. Their drummer, Paul Ravenscraft, is a talented massage therapist as well as the band's drummer. The bars and restaurants mentioned are also real, but don't expect to go to the Comet and see Desiree's butt cleavage. She, and it, don't exist. To avoid jurisdictional conflicts, I have redrawn Cincinnati police districts to include the dog park in District Five. Any deviation from proper police procedure is a product of my fevered imagination and no reflection on the Cincinnati Police Department.

P.S. In the book, Peter doesn't understand Catherine's reference to Oliver North because he's under fifty. For those of you who are also under fifty, Catherine is referring to the Iran-Contra scandal of the early Eighties. During a congressional hearing, Oliver North was asked where he got the money to pay for a $17,000 alarm system. He responded that he saved the money up in his change jar. Alma would have happily explained this to Peter, but alas, there was no good place to slip that conversation into the book.

About the Author

Carol Ann Newsome is a writer and painter who lives in Cincinnati with her three rescued dogs. She can be found every morning at the Mount Airy Dog Park. She can also be contacted at carolannnewsome@netzero.net

Books by Carol Ann Newsome

A Shot in the Bark
Drool Baby

Email carolannnewsome@netzero.net if you would like to be notified about future releases by Carol Ann Newsome

Made in the USA
San Bernardino, CA
18 December 2014